A NOVEL

WILL THE **TRUTH** SET YOU **FREE?**

HARD TRUTH

A NOVEL

WILL THE TRUTH SET YOU FREE?

ANDREW BUTTERS

STIRLING
PRESS

an imprint of
OGHMA CREATIVE MEDIA

OGHMA

C R E A T I V E   M E D I A

Stirling Press
An imprint of Oghma Creative Media, Inc.
2401 Beth Lane, Bentonville, Arkansas 72712

Library of Congress Cataloging-in-Publication Data

Names: Butters, Andrew, author.
Title: Hard Truth/Andrew Butters |
Description: First Edition. | Bentonville: Stirling, 2018.
Identifiers: LCCN: 2018942278 | ISBN: 978-1-63373-424-1 (hardcover) |
ISBN: 978-1-63373-425-8 (trade paperback) | ISBN: 978-1-63373-426-5 (eBook)
Subjects: BISAC: FICTION/Noir | FICTION/Thriller/Psychological |
FICTION/Urban
LC record available at: https://lccn.loc.gov/2018942278

Striling Press trade paperback edition November, 2018

Jacket & Interior Design by Casey W. Cowan
Editing by George "Clay" Mitchell and Gordon Bonnet

For my parents,
Donald Trump and Kevin Smith

ACKNOWLEDGEMENTS

A LOT GOES INTO WRITING a novel, even one that's not particularly long. There is a tendency to think that "anyone can do it" or the exercise would become trivial "if I had more time." That, as it turns out, could not be further from the truth. Not only is writing a novel a laborious task, it is what I like to call one of the only jobs that you do completely on your own but is impossible to do without the help of many others. While, in the end, I was the one who put the words down on the page, I required the support, guidance, and friendship of a good number of people.

My parents were educators and not only raised me to appreciate structure, form, and the value of the written word, but also how to be a decent human being, a loyal friend, and most importantly recognize when people like Thomas Van Steen were entering my field of view and how to avoid their influences. I thank them for their lifetime of support. I have yet to encounter a situation or take on a challenge where their guidance has not served me well.

I want to thank all my teachers for their dedication and commitment to learning. I also want to extend a special thank you to two of them. Mr. Sedgewick taught me science in my first year of high school and later would teach me physics. He was the reason I studied the subject in University and why my fascination with the physical world still exists today. The other teacher deserving of a special call out is my English teacher, Ms. Nowak. In the ninth grade, she gave me the worst mark I had ever received in English, and three years later, she gave me the best one. She did not merely teach me a subject, she taught me that difficult things were still possible if I wanted it badly enough and did the work.

My writing group, The Quillies, has been a source of constant support and required moments of levity. I cannot imagine a finer group of people hanging out together on Facebook. In particular, Gordon, Allison, Sami-Jo, and K.D. are four of the greatest friends a person could ask for. I would not have words in print or the desire to put more words in print if it were not for them.

Last, but certainly not least, it is of the utmost importance that I thank my wife and children. They gave me the time and space to do this. Without their sacrifices of husband and dad time, I would not have been able to do the only thing I have ever felt compelled to do—write.

PROLOGUE

MOTHER

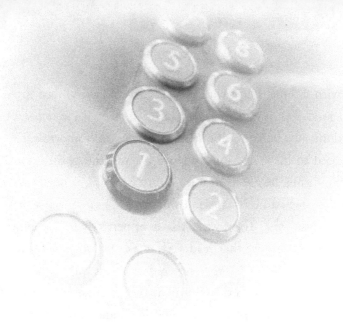

MONDAY, JULY 10, 11:30 A.M.

Thomas held his sleeping mother's hand as she lay motionless in her fancy medical bed. Her face wore an expression of pain and discomfort. Even with the oxygen mask, she had difficulty.

The nurse was singing a song and folding laundry. Sandra was putting a perfectly folded fitted sheet onto a pile of flat sheets and pillow cases forming on top of the dresser.

"Why don't you take the rest of the day off?" Thomas offered.

"That's very generous of you, sir, but it's really not necessary. Go to the office or go buy your wife something pretty, I'm sure she'll appreciate that," Sandra suggested.

"Yes, I'm sure she would, but I want to spend some time with my mother during the day for a change. How's she doing today, anyway?"

"Not great, but you know she's been having ups and downs for a while now."

"I should have expected a downturn. She had a couple good days in a row. It was probably too much to hope for her to put together one more. Go home."

"Are you quite sure?"

"Yeah, I'll be staying here for the remainder of the day and at least until Mrs. Van Steen or Brittany get back."

"As you wish. I'll just finish with this laundry and then be on my way."

"Sounds good. I'm just going to hop in the shower. If I'm not out by the time you're done, just let yourself out and we'll see you tomorrow."

He retreated to his washroom to clean up and throw on some casual clothes. It wasn't often he got to wear jeans on a Monday. When he came out of his bedroom dressed in a Hawaiian shirt and a pair of well-worn Levi's 501s, the nurse was gone. There was a basket of perfectly folded laundry on the coffee table with a note that read, *She didn't eat much breakfast so she might be hungry. There's soup in the fridge. Thank you! Sandra.*

Thomas took the note and threw it in the garbage and checked the fridge. There was a bowl of soup with a plastic lid and another note on top that read, *"For Mother."*

Thomas checked his watch and saw that it was just about time for lunch so he pulled the soup out of the fridge and microwaved it for a few minutes, which turned out to be entirely too long, as the bowl was too hot to the touch when it was done being nuked. He grabbed a dish towel from the handle of the oven door and wrapped his hands around the bowl before shuffling back the way he came with extreme caution. He didn't spill a drop.

He walked like a tightrope performer around the corner and into the room, nudging the door open with his knee. She didn't budge as he fumbled his way to her side, ensuring he took a wide berth around her bed to avoid a hot soup disaster. Setting the bowl down on the nightstand and pulling up the rocking chair, he sat down, closed his eyes, and rocked himself for a few seconds. The quiet was nice.

The cell phone in his pocket rang with the chorus to "Sweet Caroline" blasting through the faded denim. He jumped up to silence the phone and his knee caught the edge of the nightstand and knocked a glop of soup onto the hardcover copy of Dickens as well as the alarm clock. He pressed the answer button on his phone as he reached to the floor where he dropped the dishtowel after delivering the soup.

"What?" he whispered.

"Thomas? It's Roger from Doodlepants Toys and Collectibles. I have some news about your costs."

"Yeah, it's me. Just dealing with a, uh, situation here." Thomas wiped the soup off the book. "Lay it on me, how bad is it?"

"It's bad. Really bad. After your up-front capital costs for basic materials and transportation…."

Thomas flinched and bumped the bowl of soup as he was trying to clean up his mess and sent more spilling onto the alarm clock, table, and floor. "God damn it. Go on, but hurry it up. My situation got worse."

"Want me to call you back?"

"No, I need to know now."

"Well, after the up-front capital costs for basic materials and transportation it's going to cost at least three times what you budgeted for the manufacturing and distribution."

"What? Did you say *three times?*"

"At least."

"Jesus Christ. What the hell happened?"

"An earthquake. It damaged the manufacturing plant. No casualties, but no production for a while either."

"Son of a—"

"Listen, if there's any way to get out of that contract I'd find it. You'll be lucky to make a third of what you were hoping."

"Fuck."

He ended the call, slumped down in the antique rocker, put his head in his hands, and rubbed his forehead. The flashing blue light on his phone caught his attention and the little envelope icon indicated he had a voicemail. He dialed and wedged the phone between his ear and shoulder to listen to the message. As he leaned forward to mop up the soup, his hand pressed a button on the alarm clock and the radio started blasting.

"For the love of—" He scrambled to unplug the alarm clock as he listened.

"Thomas, it's Stephen. I'm still waiting for the contract. I thought Jenny was supposed to make copies and fax them over before she left the office. Get me back with the status ASAP. I'll be in class so send a text or leave a message."

He looked down at his sleeping mother with a big grin on his face. "She hasn't faxed it." His hand found a cord behind the night side table. He gave it a yank and his mother's ventilator started beeping loudly. "For fuck's sake." She stirred in the bed and he reached down and yanked the plug out of the wall for the clock and fished around for the cord to her machine. Soup was everywhere. His fingers found his target and he felt his way down the wall until they touched a wall plate. After two tries the machine's quiet hum and her labored breathing were the only sounds in the room. He checked his watch and calculated twenty minutes to get to the office—if traffic cooperated. He kissed his mother on the forehead and bolted out the door.

He waited only a minute for the elevator to arrive and in that time he left a voicemail for Jenny to not fax the contract. The elevator doors opened as he cursed Jenny for not being in the office or answering her cell phone. He stepped in and pushed the button for the lobby, the last floor for his elevator, and cursed the design of the building for having a separate elevator to take you to the parking level

He hammered on the door close button in false belief that this would result in the doors taking less time to shut. The automated voiced announced he was passing the ninth floor, the lights turned off and the elevator came to an abrupt stop. There was a moment of total darkness before the emergency light came on. "You gotta be fucking kidding me." He slammed an open hand against the elevator wall. "Fuck! Fuck fuck fuck fuck fuckity fuck fucking fuck!" He pushed the emergency call button and nothing happened. There was no beep or buzz or ringing or any indication at all that it was working.

He turned on the security monitors in the elevator and cycled through the floors until the image on the black and white monitor showed the lobby. It was a wide shot of the foyer with the security desk in the corner and Mitch out around the other side gyrating and twitching like he was having a seizure.

"Answer the call button, you worthless idiot."

He pressed the audio button and the blues-driven sounds of Keith Richards's guitar penetrated the steel box. The sound had a distinct echo, as if it were broadcasting out of a giant tin can, or say a small metal box eight-and-a-half floors above ground.

"Screw you, Mitch. You're a terrible Mick Jagger."

Mitch ran to the other side of the desk and picked up the security phone, and Thomas, watching and listening to the conversation, tried something different. He took out his cell phone and checked for a signal and was immediately disappointed. There was no cell coverage and he was out of Wi-Fi range for his unit or anyone else's. On top of that his battery was sitting at less than ten percent.

"Shit."

He closed his eyes and fought to remember if he plugged mother's machine back into the proper socket—the one hooked up to the backup power. He was so angry and flustered that he couldn't visualize where his hand was on the wall. Normally the alarm clock plugged into the regular socket so it would have been easy to tell, but with the phone call and the soup debacle both were unplugged. He furrowed his brow, squeezed his eyes closed more tightly, and rubbed his temples. Even plugged into the wrong socket the battery backup would last about half an hour.

He started to hyperventilate and his chest became tight. A bead of sweat rolled down his forehead and he pulled at the collar of his shirt. He checked his watch and his hand shook as he looked at the time. It was 12:02.

Mother had twenty-eight minutes to live.

—

Downstairs at the security station Mitch sat with his feet up on the desk. Outside, the entire block sat in chaos and disarray as the power outage knocked out the stoplights. Daylight streamed through the large glass windows of the foyer, and that combined with the emergency lights provided enough light to assuage any security concerns he had.

He took a look down at his security cameras. Every image was a bit darker but he could make out what he needed to in order to do his job. He wasn't worried. Aside from not really giving a damn, in the three years he'd been working there he hadn't had a single security-related incident.

Below a plastic plaque that read *"Elevator One"* was a black button with the words *"Talk/Listen"* etched on it. Above the button was a black and white monitor that was supposed to display the view from inside the elevator but all it showed was a garbled screen. It could have been a loose wire or something related to the power outage.

He squinted at the screen and tried to make out the shape of a body but couldn't. He pressed the talk button and all he heard was a high-pitched squeal coming from the speakers. He let go of the button and tapped the screen with the tip of his index finger. Satisfied he tried everything he could, he made a mental note to keep an eye on it. There was no way for him to tell at this point if that elevator was heading up or down to get someone waiting or if there was someone in it. He then did the only thing that seemed appropriate given the circumstances. He got out his cell phone and plugged a small set of external speakers into the headphone jack. He loaded up his favourite playlist and tapped the shuffle button. The twangy sound of Keith Richards's guitar blasted out the first few bars of "Honky Tonk Woman" and echoed through the foyer.

The security desk phone's ring broke him out of his Rolling Stones dance routine. He turned down the music, picked it up the receiver, and answered in his best work voice.

"Front desk. Security officer Mitchell speaking."

"*Is the power out?*"

It was Mrs. Parker from apartment 402. She was always calling down and complaining about this or paranoid about that. She was the catalyst for the building security upgrades last year.

"Yes ma'am, it's out in the whole building."

"*I don't feel safe. Do something.*"

Mitch stifled a sigh but couldn't avoid rolling his eyes. "Mrs. Parker, I can assure you that the security equipment is functioning even with the power out. It's running off our reserve power."

"*My outlets will only power the television for half an hour when the power goes out. What about then? Will you stand by my door? I'm not going to be safe!*"

"Outlets are running off separate backup power, Mrs. Parker. Remember, only the ones with the orange outline around them. The security cameras run off generators and will stay on for days."

"*Why won't my television stay on for days?*"

Mitch put his face into the palm of his hand. "It's a separate power source. You'll have to bring that up at the next board meeting. I'm looking at your fourth floor stairwell cameras as well as the one in the elevator waiting area. I'll be sure to keep a close eye on them until the power comes back on."

"You just see that you do."

He hung up the phone and turned his music back up to dance volume. Something flickered on the elevator monitor and he bent over and squinted at the screen. He still couldn't make out any shapes, at least none that would pass for human, among the black and white scramble. He stepped out from behind his desk and started to do his best Mick Jagger dance.

———

Thomas checked his watch. It was four past twelve. He checked his phone battery. Eight percent. He shook the device in his hand.

"Screw you, phone. Why won't you get a signal? Why is your battery draining so quickly?"

He mustered a vague memory about cell phones and prolonging battery use, but was never more than a few feet away from a charging cable though so he couldn't recall the information he needed. He used the back of his hand to rub away the sweat that was starting to collect on his forehead. His hands made fists and then he rubbed his clammy palms. Holding his stomach as he bent over at the waist, he kept his breathing short and shallow. With squinted eyes he struggled to focus, kept still, and stared at the video monitor on the elevator panel above the rows of buttons with floor numbers on them. He furrowed his brow and then raised his eyebrows and opened his eyes as wide as they could go. Something wasn't right. He pressed the talk button again. It didn't work. He had only been stuck in the elevator for four minutes.

The light changed on the marble foyer floor as one of the main lobby doors opened. He moved his head closer to the monitor. It was his wife, Brenda. She would have to walk up twenty-four flights of stairs but even in her three-thousand-dollar Jimmy Choo shoes it wouldn't take her twenty-six minutes to make the trek up to the penthouse.

Thomas pressed the talk button one more time and yelled into the tiny void of the elevator. He swore in frustration when it became apparent that neither Mitch nor Brenda could hear his cries for help. Thomas couldn't speak, so he decided to listen and pressed the button labelled "Audio" beside the monitor displaying the lobby.

Mitch was in front of the desk dancing or convulsing, Thomas couldn't much tell from his vantage point, but the Van Halen song "Panama" echoed through the lobby so he suspected he witnessed Mitch's version of dancing. Brenda walked over to him and tapped him on the shoulder.

"Good morning, Mitch."

Mitch let out a high-pitched squeal, jumped, and spun around. His right hand reached down to the holster at his waist.

"Jesus, Mrs. Van Steen, you just about scared the pants off me."

Brenda looked down at Mitch's hand and smiled.

"Well, at least you didn't shoot me."

Mitch took his hand off his holster and folded his arms across his chest.

"The power's out, so you'll have to take the stairs. The emergency lights are on, though."

"Is my husband home?"

"I think so." He checked his watch. "Your nurse left about half an hour ago and I haven't seen him come or go all day."

"Hmm. Thank you, Mitch. Keep an eye on me on your little cameras there in case I fall and you need to come rescue me."

Thomas swore she saw Brenda wink before she walked away. He tried to focus his eyes on the monitor but they were starting to water. Brenda headed in the direction of the West stairwell, opened the door, and slipped through an opening barely wide enough for her to get through. He pressed the down arrow button on the panel beside the monitor labelled *"West Stair."* It toggled through the floors starting with the one he was closest to, and he caught up with his wife by the time she rounded the corner to reach the second floor.

He pressed the up arrow beside his monitor and followed her up floor-by-floor. He was stuck between eleven and twelve and would have to wait until then before raising a ruckus. It was a Hail Mary even to try, since the elevators were in the center of the building and the west stairwell was down the end of the hall, but he had to try something.

Brenda walked around the corner for the third floor. He pressed the up arrow. Four. Up arrow. Five. Up arrow and then she stopped. He straightened his head and peered at the monitor. She was fishing around in her purse for something and after a few seconds of searching came out with her cell phone. Thomas pushed the audio button beside the monitor just as Brenda answered the call.

"Hello?"

He turned his head so his ear was closer to the speaker.

"Oh, Anthony, that's wonderful news! You see, I knew it would all work out. I guess Stephen's reminder to Jenny worked after all?"

Thomas stared at the screen and blinked twice. "What the actual fuck?" He leaned back and put his ear to the speaker.

"I'm just on my way up to the apartment. Unfortunately, Thomas is home. At least that's according to the security guard in the lobby." She paused as Anthony spoke. "What kind of celebration?" She paused to let Anthony respond. "Oh my. You're making me blush." She paused again. "No, I won't take off my underwear and drive back to you commando."

Thomas punched the monitor with his fist. The screen spider-webbed and shards of glass dug into his knuckles. He paid no attention to the pain or the blood and ran his hands through his hair. He paced back and forth in the elevator like a prisoner deprived of yard time and returned his attention to the conversation between his wife and contractor.

"How about I drive back and you can take the underpants off for me?" There was another moment of silence. "It's a deal then. Congratulations, sweetie. I'll see you in twenty minutes." Brenda put the phone back in her purse and headed back downstairs.

"No! Go back upstairs, you cheating whore!" He pounded on the talk button. "Don't you dare go back down, Brenda. Brenda? Brenda, get your ass back upstairs!"

She reached the bottom and headed back out into the lobby. Mitch was out in front of the security desk again dancing away and singing along to

David Bowie's "Space Oddity." He saw her come out of the door and looked over at the desk he promised to be sitting behind when she went upstairs a few minutes ago. He stood up straight as she approached. She dug into her purse, opened her wallet, and took out a hundred dollar bill and handed it to him. "Make sure you forget you saw me this morning, okay?"

Mitch took the bill and stuffed it in his front pocket. "Yes, ma'am. Never saw you."

"Perfect. Thank you, Mitchell."

Thomas fell backwards onto the wall of the elevator and his head bounced off the floor-to-ceiling mirrors. "If you get caught cheating, our prenup says you don't get two-fifths of sweet fuck all, Brenda." He checked his watch. It was ten after twelve.

*PART*ONE

STEPHEN, BRENDA & ANTHONY

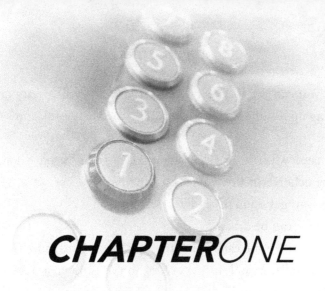

*CHAPTER*ONE

Stephen was a short man with thin shoulders, pointy elbows, and a ferocious comb over. He sat in a leather guest chair and picked at his cuticles. He suspected the chair alone cost more than one of his mortgage payments. The monstrosity looked like it would swallow him at any second and his knee bounced up and down in quick staccato pulses. His business partner, Thomas, if you could call him that, was on the phone with someone who, based on the end of the conversation he could hear, was not his wife.

"Listen, babe, I'm going to have to call you back, all right?" There was a pause and then a high-pitched squeal. Thomas moved the receiver away from his ear and when the squealing subsided put the phone back in the crook of his neck. "Listen, babe… babe… babe, *listen.*"

His voice rose with each syllable. He pressed the mute button and muttered expletives directed at no one in particular. Stephen folded his hands in his lap and looked over his right shoulder out at the vast expanse of New York City. He tried to envision what the home of the mistress of a wealthy businessman looked like.

Unmute. "No, I'm sorry I raised my voice, it's just that I have a client here and it's important…." Pause. "No, you're important too. It's just that…." Pause. "I understand." Pause. "I love you too, babe. I'll be over after I hit

the gym so you can get all sweaty and wet after I get all sweaty and wet."
Thomas hung up his phone, raised both his hands palms up, and shrugged.
"Chicks, eh?"

"Yeah, I hate it when they get all up in my grill like that," Stephen deadpanned.

Laughter echoed off the windows of the large corner office. "Did you
seriously just say 'get up in my grill'?"

"It's urban. I can be urban."

"No, Stephen. No you can't be urban. You're about as urban as John Deere.
You're a wet noodle, man, but that's okay. You've got a great idea and we're
going to make a green and yellow truck full of money together. Then we'll
get you a protein shake, a gym membership, and a high-priced whore. You'll
look and feel like a million bucks!"

"Only a million?"

"Now that's the fucking spirit, Steve-O! Smack the table and yell it."

He shrank into the chair. "What?"

Thomas slammed both hands down on the mahogany desk. "Only a
million?" He brought his hands down onto the hard surface again, this time with
a loud smack that shook the Tiffany lamp and elicited a flinch from Stephen.
"Only a million? Come on, do it, Steve. Show me what you're made of!"

Stephen reached out and smacked his palms down on the hard surface.
"Only a million?" He sat back with a concerned look, staring down at his palms.

"Don't worry, buddy, the cleaning ladies do a great job here. The best job.
Now look here at the contracts and tell me what you think."

He slid a small stack of legal-sized papers across the desk and Stephen
flipped through them with surprising speed.

"Holy shit, man, are you reading them or just counting the pages?"

"I can speed read." His eyes never left the stack of papers.

"Might want to take your time with those, this is a big risk we're taking."

He looked up from the papers and the two men locked eyes. "I know. It's
my life's savings."

"Your life's savings is just a squirt of piss in an ocean full of it. No offense,
but you're not exactly living uptown, if you know what I mean."

"That may be true and from a risk perspective this little enterprise is akin to you heading over to Atlantic City and playing the nickel slots on your lunch break. If this deal goes sour you have to forgo a golf trip down to Florida to make up for it. Me? I will lose everything! My house. My car. Probably my wife. I'll have to work ten hours a day for the rest of my life to make it all back. Do you know what they pay teachers in New York City? Do you know? They pay them shit fuck all, that's what they pay us. And I don't teach chemistry, so I can't even fall back on that."

The reference to Breaking Bad flew over the businessman's head. Who needs television when you can look out at the skyscraper cityscape of New York and imagine the glory of Thomas Van Steen, Esquire, and all-around asshole? There was silence for several seconds before the breath of a long sigh carrying remnants of stale cigarettes wafted across the desk.

"What would it take to get you to sign that paper today, Stephen? Forget rules, forget exactly how much capital each person is investing. Forget all that. What changes would you make that would put your signature on the bottom before you leave today?"

"Shouldn't we get our lawyers in here for this?"

"Screw the lawyers. Screw 'em. We talked ad nauseam with those money-grubbing Jews for weeks, didn't we? And what did it get us?"

Silence.

"I'll tell you what it got us. It got us shit fuck all, if I can borrow your turn of phrase? So screw the lawyers. Screw the rules. Tell me what has to happen to get your signature on the bottom so I can get out of here and go visit my lady friend I had on the phone there a minute ago."

Stephen pushed the chair out from the massive desk and placed the gold pen at the bottom of the page, the tip pointing at the signature line at the bottom. He stood up and stretched, narrowing his eyes.

"I can appreciate where you're coming from on this, I really can. You've definitely put more money in to start so it's only fair you get more return. It's really what comes after that I'm interested in. You want to make a quick buck."

"You're damn right I do."

"I get it, and I'm more than happy with that, but what happens after that initial deal? You have this thing drawn up like we'd be equal partners and we both know that's not true. You've contributed more up front, and done more to line up the initial deal, but after that we both know your involvement is going to be limited."

"Now hang on a second—"

"Listen, you don't know the space. You don't understand the technology. You can't even speak the right language. That's where I come in. That's where forty-five years of being a nerd enters the equation."

Thomas folded his arms and pursed his lips, clearly not impressed with the sudden growth of brass testicles sprouting from between Stephen's legs. Stephen didn't stop.

"You want to know what it will take to get me to sign on the dotted line?"

"Please, enlighten me."

He sat back down in the chair and pressed down on his comb over.

"I simply want more."

"Oh, do you?"

Unflinching, Stephen picked up the pen and flipped back a few pages in the contract. He crossed out a number and wrote in a new one. He initialed the change, turned the contract around, and slid it across the desk. He looked up to see if there was any noteworthy expression staring back at him. All he saw was a cold, emotionless visage and a ridiculous toupee. He stood up and extended his arm to hand the gargoyle the pen.

He took it and raised one eyebrow and tapped the pen on the desk. Tap, tap, tap. Tap, tap, tap.

"Look, we both know that once the ink is dry on the first client contract you're going to turn into an absentee parent, divorced from all that's going on and barely showing up on time for the Christmas concert, price tag still on the gift you picked up at the convenience store around the corner. Take your money and run. Let me do the heavy lifting."

Tap, tap, tap. Thomas flipped back one page and scratched out the proposed changes, wrote in changes of his own, and initialed beside each one. He stood and spun the stack of papers around and slid it across the desk. He lay the pen down on top, Van Steen company logo facing up.

Stephen took the pen, initialed the changes, and with his eyes locked on Thomas's, he turned to the back page and signed the bottom.

For the first time in weeks, Thomas smiled.

"Jenny!"

The office door opened to reveal a young woman in her early twenties, wearing a sheer blouse and a mini skirt that didn't leave much to the imagination. Both men fought the urge to gawk and lost, but only one of them would feel bad about it later. As she floated toward the desk, Stephen turned his attention to the stack of papers. Thomas turned his attention to Jenny.

"Jenny, can you please sign the bottom and go make copies? And grab some champagne from the fridge. Stephen and I have to celebrate our new agreement."

"Our copier is broken." She lowered her chin and raised her eyebrows. The copier had broken the other day during some impromptu, and rather active, sex between the two of them. "I'll be running downstairs to use the one in Accounts Payable before I leave tonight."

She grabbed the stack of papers off the desk and turned to leave.

"Will there be anything else?"

"See to it those pages get faxed to Stephen after you make the copies, and bring the champagne like I told you to." Thomas made sure to take a nice long look at Jenny as she walked back to the door. He waited for it to close before turning his attention back to Stephen. "Now that is one seriously fine piece of ass."

She returned a few seconds later with the champagne and he gave her a wink and then poured two glasses. Raising his in the air he toasted the new agreement. "To making a ton of money!"

"I'll definitely drink to that." Stephen took his first-ever sip of champagne.

FRIDAY, JULY 7, 6:00 P.M.

The Van Steen penthouse was the only unit on the top floor of the building, and the elevator opened into a big foyer adorned with lavish pieces of art and a water feature. By the letter of the building bylaws, the space in front of the elevators was "public" and Thomas saw to it that all the décor and design work came out of the condo fees. Decorating the space as she saw fit was his anniversary present to his wife five years ago. Every year since, she made one significant change to the space. This year she added the water feature. He exited the elevator and walked toward his door and heard his daughter, Brittany, yelling.

"Jesus, Mom, it's not like we don't have the money. It's not like I'm asking for my own private island. Fuck!"

"First of all, watch your mouth, young lady. Second, we agreed to finance your school provided you met certain conditions. *One*—you don't get a car, *two*—you get a small—very small—allowance to cover coffee and fast food, and *three*—you get a credit card with no cash advance privilege and the bill goes to your father at his office, and he reads it every month in great detail. You aren't meeting them. Therefore, we don't owe you so much as half a sweet potato pie."

"You're being unreasonable. I'm just asking for a favor."

"And this is how you ask for a favor? You take the Lord's name in vain and spew filth at your mother?"

Thomas threw his keys into the crystal bowl on the small antique phone table by the door. "Hello, family. My, isn't it nice to see and hear everyone getting along so swimmingly."

Both women turned to face him but Brittany spoke out before her mother could get a word in.

"Daddy, mom's being unreasonable—again."

"From what I could hear you were doing nothing but disrespecting both our agreement and your mother."

"You talk to her like that all the time! You don't think I can hear you, but I can. You treat her like shit."

Thomas grabbed her by the wrist, gave her a slight twist, and caused her arm to bend at an awkward angle.

"Fuck! Ow!"

Brenda stepped in between the two and put her hand on Thomas's.

"That's quite enough, both of you! We'll have no more of this crazy talk, potty mouth, or arm twisting. Brittany, you sit down with your father and explain to him why you need to break our agreement. Thomas, just so it's clear, the only answer you are to provide is 'no.' Do you understand me?"

"Yes, dear."

Thomas dragged Brittany by her arm and led her into the kitchen and directed her into a chair. He sat in the chair opposite and folded his arms across his chest.

"Quit your bellyaching. Now what is it you want? More money? A new car? Crown jewels?"

"You never give me anything! We're rich as hell and you don't give me shit."

"Is that so? Since birth you've eaten the finest food outside of a five-star restaurant, been dressed in the trendiest and most fashionable clothes, vacationed all over the world, slept in the most comfortable bed money can buy, had every techno gadget your heart desires, haven't paid a cent for any of it or even been asked to pitch in. PLUS, you're twenty years old and going to college that we're paying for and haven't even had to spend a dime on books or even so much as a single latte from the coffee shop. You get things, not cash. That's the deal. These things don't get lost or misplaced and sold for cash. You don't ask for cash. You get that when you earn it. Get a goddamn job and then you can have goddamn cash."

"Language, Thomas!"

He put his head in his hands and whispered, "Jesus Christ on a cracker."

Brittany let out a giggle snort. "So what I'm hearing is that you think I'm a spoiled brat and you're not giving me money."

"Someone's been paying attention in her classes on how to have a conversation using active listening. Well done."

"Huh? What's active listening?"

"It's what you did there with the 'what I'm hearing' thing." He ran his hands through his thinning hair. "It's just that… you know what? Never mind. You're right. You've been spoiled for far too long and we're not going to give you money. We'll support you in whatever you want to do, especially if that whatever ends up being a job. Something you will never get if you can't bother to put on something other than yoga pants."

"What's wrong with yoga pants?"

"Do you realize those pants leave nothing to the imagination? I have to look away every time you walk by. People shouldn't be privy to whether or not you're wearing any underpants. If you aren't they will think you're a slut and if you are it's absolutely none of their business as to what kind."

Brittany rolled her eyes as only an exasperated daughter can and let out a muffled "harrumph."

"So no, you're not getting any money. Not today, not until your mother and I both die. Which if genetics have any say in it won't be for a long, long time. Speaking of which, have you checked on your grandmother lately?"

Brenda walked into the kitchen, putting in her earrings. "I checked on her before little Miss here tried to treat me like an ATM. The nurse should be here any minute. Now get on your tux and shave. You look like a damn Wall Street hobo."

He stood up, slumped his shoulders, and untucked one side of his shirt. "Yes, dear."

"And stop *saying* that! For cryin' in the sink, you'd think I was some sort of abusive battleaxe."

He dragged his feet across the apartment carpet and peered in to check on his mother. Her chest rose and fell slowly. The only sound was the soft whish and whir of the ventilator and the hum of the other machines among the cords and cables beside her antique bed her own mother slept in when she was born more than ninety seven years ago.

"Mother?" he whispered, and then again little louder, "Mother?" No response. He snuck into the room to her bedside and put his hand on her forehead. She was warm but not too warm. He tiptoed away and wondered if she was just faking it so he wouldn't have to see the pain on her face from having heard the screaming on the other side of the condo. She may have been old and dying, but she could still hear a mouse fart across the room and some of the time her brain fired on all cylinders.

He wandered back to his bedroom to shave and put on his tux and came out to the foyer just as his daughter was leaving and the nurse was coming in. "Where are you going?"

"Out. Unless you've put a freeze on my credit card, too."

"That can be arranged."

Her mother shook the nurse's hand. "I don't know how long we're going to be, but let's just assume it will be late. Help yourself to anything from the fridge and the remote for the TV is on the armrest of Thomas's hideous chair in the corner."

The nurse held up a large canvas bag filled with yarn. "Not a problem, I've got my Velda Brotherton romance novel and my knitting to keep me busy. How's she been lately?"

"Not bad. Probably on the good side of neutral. Just make sure she's plugged in to the backup power outlet, just in case," said Brenda.

"Of course, Mrs. Van Steen. I know the drill. You go enjoy yourselves. We'll be just fine here, as always."

In the elevator, Brittany set all the security monitors to the ground floor. The lobby was empty except for the security guard sitting at his desk reading a book. "Do you think he knows people are watching him all the time?"

"I don't like those things. Not one bit. It's an invasion of privacy, that's what they are," Brenda said.

"I dunno." Brittany leaned in closer. "I kind of think they're interesting. Like, this one time, I saw the Millers from apartment 404 holding hands as they walked up the stairs together. Mr. Miller was telling a story about one of his buddies from 'the club' and Mrs. Miller was laughing her ass off. It was really cute. Totally candid. Completely unscripted. Like real life unfolding right in front of you."

Thomas shoved his hands into his pockets. "Well, someone better think it's worth it, for what the setup cost everyone."

At the ground floor the trio walked into the foyer where Mitch was entering names from the log book into the computer.

"Oh, hello, Van Steens, let me get you a cab. One, two, or three?"

"Two, please."

Brittany never passed up the opportunity to contradict her father, especially in front of people she knew he felt were beneath him.

"Actually, just one. I'll hike to the subway and cab home, or maybe crash on Sam's couch."

"Like hell you will!"

Brenda put her hand on his arm.

"Relax, dear. Sam's a girl. Samantha. I know her mother from back when Brit was in high school. They played on the field hockey team together. Isn't that right, Brittany?"

"Yeah, that's her. No need for all the drama, dad," she answered after the slightest delay. Her dad didn't look convinced, but he exhaled and the red colour started to fade from his cheeks. The cab arrived and he was the first one in.

FRIDAY, JULY 7, 8:00 P.M.

At the gala, Brenda feigned surprise when she and her husband found they had secured a spot at one of the host sponsor's tables, a construction company out of Long Island that did a lot of work building affordable housing in various parts of the United States as well as impoverished areas around the world.

They took their seats at the table and Thomas leaned over and spoke to her out of the corner of his mouth. "How exactly did we get involved with this, anyway?"

She put her hand on top of his, scanned the room, and pretended to be looking for someone. "I told you, honey. Anthony DiMarco, from DiMarco Construction and Contracting, is the man we hired to do the renovations on the beach house. His company is involved with Helping Homes, the charity throwing this gala."

"DiMarco, eh? I wonder if he knows Mikey Vee."

"Don't be racist. Not every Italian knows every other Italian in this city. And not all of them are mob either, so shut your trap about it and play nice."

"An Italian construction company out of Long Island. I'm not sure I can hold the stereotypes at bay all by myself."

"Shh. Here they come." They both stood and Brenda leaned in and gave Anthony a kiss on each cheek. "Anthony, so good to see you! Where's Angela tonight?"

"She wasn't feeling well, I'm afraid, so you all will have to settle for my partner, and my brother, Nick." Nick wore the look of a fish that has not seen water for quite some time. He pulled at his collar before he extended his hand out. Brenda held her hand as if she expected him to kiss it but he took her hand in his and gave it a firm construction worker's shake instead.

"Oh. My. That's quite a grip you've got there, Nick."

"I'm used to working with big tools." He shot a sideways glance over at his brother.

"I'll bet you are. Where are my manners? Anthony, Nick, Mr. and Mrs. Dewar, this is my husband Thomas. Thomas, Anthony and Nick are of course the ones remodelling our beach house, and the Dewars are the founders of the Healthy Home organization."

"Pleased to meet you." Mr. Dewar extended his hand to Thomas. "Let me guess, you lost a coin toss and got dragged to a stuffy fundraiser when you'd rather be watching the game?"

Thomas let a genuine laugh escape. "Nothing like that. Though I'd rather be playing poker if I'm being one hundred percent honest."

Brenda smacked him on the shoulder. "Thomas!"

Mr. Dewar waggled a celery stick with a glob of hummus on the end in Brenda's direction. "Oh, cut him a bit of slack, I know I'd rather be out with the boys tonight too—and this is my event."

The two women shook their heads while Nick's bobbed silently in the affirmative. Dinner proceeded without any further incidents and dancing began after a few speeches. Thomas checked his watch. He had less than an hour to make it to his poker game. In an attempt to get away from any further awkwardness he stood up and extended his hand to his wife. "If you'll all excuse us for a few minutes, I am going to steal my wife for a dance."

Everyone at the table nodded and smiled and he led his wife out to the dance floor.

"Well, this is unexpected."

The band started into a tango.

"I had to get away from that table."

"Oh, and I'm just the excuse. Thanks for that." A little more under her breath she added, "Asshole." Brenda turned to walk back to the table and Thomas took her by the arm and pulled her toward him as she spun around.

He grabbed her by the hip and started into the tango.

"Oh, get over yourself, Brenda, let's just enjoy a dance. I haven't forgotten those lessons from twenty years ago before our wedding. Have you?"

"How could I forget? You were three sheets to the wind for every one of them, including our wedding night. I've still got a crooked toe from you stomping on my foot."

"You still haven't learned to follow my lead."

"You're a dick."

At that moment Anthony tapped Thomas on the shoulder. "Do you mind if I cut in?"

"Not at all." Brenda responded a little too quickly for Thomas's liking but he bowed out of the dance without a response and swung by the bar and ordered a scotch with a single ice cube.

"Make it a double." The bartender poured him a double and he didn't even attempt to hide his ogling as he accepted the drink and slid a twenty across the bar. "Keep the change, beautiful." The bartender winked before turning around and his eyes didn't leave her rear end until he turned to walk away from the bar.

Alone at the table with his double scotch he leaned back and surveyed the room. There were so many people with so much money all wandering around and giving it away. It boggled his mind as he sat brooding and sipping his drink. He looked over at the dance floor saw his wife dancing with Anthony. They were hip to hip and cheek to cheek and she kept whispering something into his ear. He took a good long sip of his drink and kept his eye on them. They were laughing now, and Brenda's hand came up to the base of Anthony's neck as his hand dipped further down the small of her back.

"Fuck it." He downed the remainder of his scotch, grabbed his tux jacket, and headed for the door.

*CHAPTER*TWO

Thomas snuck into his apartment with his bag of cash. Brenda was flopped on the couch, passed out and still in her dress from the night before. One of her stilettos was by the door and the other near the entrance to the kitchen. Her clutch purse was wedged between the couch cushions with twenty dollar bills poking out of the top in what must have been a haphazard attempt to pay the cab driver and exit the taxi at the same time. He meandered toward the couch and got within three feet before he could tell that she was still drunk.

Still wired from his big poker win, Thomas didn't figure that sleep was coming anytime soon so he moved his wife's legs over and plopped himself down on the couch beside her. She smacked her chops and brushed her face with her hand like a cat grooming itself but otherwise didn't even acknowledge his presence. He preferred the company of something saucy on the internet and a hand-rolled smoke more than the stale alcohol stench of his unconscious wife, so he retreated to the bedroom for a well-deserved celebration and cigar out on the patio, not necessarily in that order.

Thomas wasn't five minutes into his cigar when an alarm bell blasted from the other side of the apartment and sent his heart into fits and his Cuban to the ground. It took him a couple seconds to register what was happening before he realized that it was one of his mother's machines screaming for attention.

He bolted towards his mother's room, hurdling over the end table by the couch as Brenda sat up and rubbed her eyes in a failed attempt to get her wits about her. He grabbed the wall to help him swing around the corner. When he reached his mother's room it wasn't immediately clear what the problem was. She had rolled over onto her side and there were several lights flashing on her ventilator.

He made his way to her side and carefully rolled her onto her back and discovered that her breathing mask had slipped off her mouth and pinched when she had rolled over. The electrode on her finger clamp detected a dip in her oxygen levels. The ventilator detected something was amiss and was the cause of all the commotion. He breathed a sigh of relief at the fact that each piece of equipment was doing its job. With the mask properly secured the machines stopped their wailing and the color returned to his mother's face. He sat down in the rocking chair beside the bed, put his head in his hands, and tried to slow his breathing. When he managed to get his heart rate and breathing back under control he stroked his mother's forehead.

Brenda stumbled into the doorway and steadied herself on the frame. One hand wiped her brow and the other clung to the doorknob like her life depended on it. "Is she okay?"

Thomas raised his head and his eyes met hers. "Yeah, she just rolled over onto her mask and the machines did their job and went batshit crazy. She's breathing normally again. Me, not so much. On the upside, at least we know how quickly I can make it to her bedroom from ours. Also, I can apparently hurdle small tables without killing myself."

"On the other upside she was strong enough to roll herself over, too."

"She hasn't been able to do that for quite a while."

Brenda turned to walk out of the room and muttered, "Maybe she feels better when you're not around."

He stood up, exited the room, and closed the door behind him. "What was that?"

"Nothing. I'm glad she's okay. And where the heck did you go last night? One second I was dancing with Anthony, the next you're at the bar staring at the bartender's chest, and then poof, you disappear without even so much as a wave."

"I left you the checkbook."

"Which I used, thank you very much. A lot." He winced and she leaned in to smell the front of his shirt.

"What do you smell? Smoke? Perfume?" He rolled his eyes back and covered his face with his hands, walked over to his black leather recliner, and threw himself into it. "This, coming from the woman I left dancing cheek-to-cheek with a member of the Mafioso AND who was sprawled on the couch passed out drunk not wearing any underpants when I got home?"

"Well darn, I really like that pair. They matched this bra perfectly. I must have taken them off when I was in the washroom and forgotten to put them back on." She pointed to the paper bag on the coffee table. "What's with the trash?"

Thomas turned on the seventy inch 4k LED television to *ESPN* to catch the scores from the West Coast games. "Open it. Convince me you weren't inappropriate with Anthony there and I might just let you have some."

She gave him the finger and reached down and looked in the bag. "I see. Did you win this at poker?"

"No, I decided I'd knock off a couple banks on my way home. Where else do you think I would get that kind of cash in a few hours?"

"I don't even want to think about the possibilities." She picked up a pile of hundreds and twenties and let the bills fall into her lap. "How much is here?"

"How big a check did you write last night?"

"I can't remember exactly. Ten or fifteen grand. We may be the proud new owners of an original oil painting by some godawful Scandinavian artist I've never heard of. I think it was a landscape with a robot on a swing or something like that."

"Oh for Christ's sake. Well, you'll be happy to hear that I won that much at poker."

"How illegal is it, exactly?"

"What do you mean, 'How illegal is it?' It's illegal. I'm not a lawyer and I don't know what the penalty is for being involved in illegal gambling. I'm just pretty sure that you can't walk into someone's house with a thousand bucks, give a cut to the hostess who runs the game, and walk out with fifteen five and not have it be against the law."

"Hold the phone. There's fifteen thousand dollars in here?"

"Fifteen-five."

"Holy cow, Thomas, I'll be honest. I didn't think you were that spectacular a poker player up until now, but fifteen grand at poker? Wow. Why don't you go to Vegas more often?"

"Fifteen-five. Your unwavering support and confidence is what makes it all worthwhile."

"Well it's true! Daddy Van Steen handed you a fortune and thankfully an accountant to go with it. You've bounced from one scheme to another over the last two decades and barely increased our net worth. What kind of ROI is that? Maye that's what I should have carved into your tombstone. 'Here lies Thomas Gordon Van Steen. He didn't make it any worse.'"

"I've been successful, Brenda, and you've got the Jimmy Choos to prove it, so get off my case. I just happen to be the best at taking a bunch of suckers for a thousand bucks every few months, that's all."

"Wait a second, how many times have you come home with a brown bag full of cash, and where the hell have you been stashing it? It's not under the mattress, is it? That'd be too cliché even for my tastes."

"I don't know, maybe a dozen times over the last couple years."

"Including tonight?"

"Something like that. I'm not too sure to be honest. I have a safe place for it, don't worry."

"Just curious, but why are you telling me all of this now?"

Thomas thought about it for a few seconds. "I'm not sure. Probably because I wanted you to see that I was out having a grand old time raking in the dough and maybe a little to show that I have cash just lying around and you can't have any of it."

"Nice. I see winning at poker hasn't made you any less of an asshole."

"Hey, I liked the idea of having a safety deposit box filled to the brim with cash that no one knew about. It felt like I was in a Robert Ludlum novel."

"Since we're all being honest here I should inform you that I'm taking a bunch of this for later today, and I'm going shopping. You reminded me that I want to pay a visit to my good friend Jimmy Choo. I should probably go get some new underwear, too." She grabbed the bag of cash, emptied what she estimated was half onto the coffee table, picked up the bag, and walked toward the bedroom.

He looked down at the pile of money on the table and his brow furrowed. From the bedroom he heard his wife. "And I'm finishing the cigar you left out on the patio."

He reached into his jacket pocket, slid the other cigar out, and bit the end off. Picking up a hundred dollar bill he lit Ben Franklin's head with his monogrammed lighter and touched it to the end of his Cuban cigar.

SATURDAY, JULY 8, 9:00 A.M.

Brenda woke with no one beside her. She snuck down the hall and peered around the corner. *SportsCenter* was on and Thomas was asleep on the couch. The butt of his cigar was sticking out of the top of a rocks glass that had a putrid brown liquid and pieces of charred tobacco at the bottom. She wandered back to the bedroom and hopped in the shower.

After she toweled off, she put on her favourite blue dress, did a quick number on her hair, and put on a bit of makeup. She grabbed an appropriate purse for her excursion out of her expansive walk-in closet and eyed the brown paper bag of money sitting on her night side table. The top drawer of her make-up table was home to a handful of black hair elastics which were perfect for wrapping the bills. It didn't take long before all the hundreds were in one pile, the fifties in another, and twenties in another.

There was a total of nine thousand four hundred and sixty dollars. She stacked the bills on top of each other with the twenties on the bottom and the hundreds on the top, and wrapped the hair elastic around the stack. Satisfied with her work, she stuffed the wad of cash into her purse and left to go shopping. Her first stop was to pick up a pair of shoes, followed by a trip to the lingerie store. She didn't take long to find a suitable match for the ones that went missing the night before, and a few other items she thought were cute.

She locked the door to the change room, fished her cell phone out of her Louis Vuitton handbag, and thumbed through her contacts until she found

Contractor. "Hey, Anthony, I just bought some spiffy new Choos and some sexy underwear to replace the pair I left in the men's room last night. Are you busy?"

"What are chews? Some fancy new exotic bubble gum?"

"Not 'chews.' *'Choos.'* Jimmy Choo. He makes shoes. Fabulous ones. Is this seriously what you're focused on right now?"

"Right, no. Of course not. You said something about you wanting to leave underwear on the floor of my bathroom after we have sex."

"No, you doofus, I bought new underwear to replace…."

Anthony cut her off with a fit of laughter.

"Oh, very funny, jerk. You know, I have a good mind to not come over and show you my new panties, after all. I put them on and they look fantastic. I'm actually calling you from the dressing room in the store."

"Pic or it didn't happen, gorgeous."

"You dirty little pervert. You're lucky I'm feeling playful." Brenda stood in front of the mirror and held up her camera, making sure she got her underpants in the shot, tucked in her belly, and propped her boobs up in her bra. She pressed the camera button on her phone and the flash triggered as her phone made the camera shutter sound. "Oh, poo. Hang on." She changed the camera settings to not use the flash and took another picture. The artificial shutter sound echoed through the change rooms. Satisfied with the result, she selected *Anthony* as the contact and pressed *send.* "There. Check your text messages."

"Nothing there."

"Huh." Brenda looked at her text messages and there was an outgoing message from her a few seconds ago.

"Check the number," he said.

"Okay, hang on." She tapped the name *Contractor* on her screen and it took her to Anthony's contact information on her phone. Beside the email address *info@dimarcoconstruction.com* was the word *Default* in parenthesis. "Yeah, I accidentally sent it as an email and not a text. That's weird. I must have messed it up when I was drunk last night."

"I'll check my email now."

Brenda heard him walking across a wood floor followed by hysterical laughter. It was so loud she was sure people in the other stalls could hear it.

"Seriously? You're *laughing* at me? This does not bode well for you getting to see me in those later, you know that, right?"

"No, no, no. It's not that. It's just that you sent the picture to info at Dimarco Construction dot com *instead of* Anthony at Dimarco Construction dot com."

"Oh, would you look at that. And this is somehow funny?" Brenda crooked the phone in her neck and tried to get her pants back on without falling over.

"Yeah." He stifled another chuckle. *"The 'info' email address goes to me, my brother, and our secretary all at the same time."*

Brenda dropped the phone on the ground. "Shit." She bent down and picked up the phone. "Are you kidding me? Please tell me you're just being a jerk right now so I don't have to completely die of embarrassment."

"Sorry, sweetheart. I'm afraid you just showed my brother and our secretary your assets."

"Anthony, that's not funny!"

"It's a little funny. Look, it's no problem. I'll just call my brother right now and tell him to delete the message without opening it. He won't ask any questions. Well, none I can't explain away at least."

"Are you sure?"

"Positive, sweetness. I promise it'll be fine. Trust me."

"Fine, but what about your secretary? What if your brother has already seen the message? Oh, my god, this is so embarrassing. Plus everyone is going to know that we're having an affair. I think I'm going to be sick."

"Listen, sweetness, just breathe. In and out really slow."

Brenda took a few deep breaths in through her nose and out her mouth. She fanned herself with her free hand.

"There you go. Just take nice slow breaths. You'll be fine. My brother is in the car for the next few hours and he doesn't have a fancy smartphone. So he won't be checking his email. I'll take care of it."

"What is it with you two and your archaic technology anyway? You probably have a dot matrix printer at the office, too."

"Hey, if it ain't broke. And speaking of the office, our secretary doesn't arrive until Monday morning. I'll whip over to the office tomorrow and log into the computer and delete the email."

Brenda exhaled for a six count and her jaw began to unclench. "I hope you're right, Anthony."

"Of course I'm right, sweetness. I fix things, remember? That's what I do."

"Well, you can fix me a drink because I'll be over shortly and I need something to take the edge off."

"Sure thing. See you soon."

"See you soon."

She ended the call, stepped out of the change room, and walked to the nearby cash register to pay. The cashier wore a strange smirk on her face and refused to make eye contact with her as she rang up her purchases. On her way out the door, she glanced back and saw her erupting into a fit of laughter.

SATURDAY, JULY 8, 9:45 A.M.

At Anthony's small but very beautiful house in the suburbs of New Jersey, Brenda parked in his driveway and walked into the house without knocking. He had just started a phone call and was waiting for the person on the other end to pick up. He motioned to Brenda to have a seat.

"Hey, Nick, it's me. No, ma's fine. I'm fine. Everyone's fine. I gotta favor to ask though and I need you to not ask any questions about it." There was a short pause and Brenda noticed Anthony biting his nails. She'd never seen him do that before. "I'm sorry if that's a little too cryptic for you, but I need you to trust me, and it's not even that big a deal but I think I just emailed you a computer virus or something. Give me your email password so I can log in and delete it before you check it." There was another short pause and another nail bite. "What if Diane goes into your email or something? If she hops on the computer and just clicks on it seeing it's from me, she won't think twice and then you're fucked." Brenda scowled at his use of the swearword, then softened her expression realizing she, too, swore in the last hour over this very same problem. "Yeah, I know I make a lot of sense for a guy who just emailed his brother a computer virus. What's the damn password?"

Anthony grabbed a pen from the desk and scribbled down the password. He opened a web browser and logged into his brother's email account. There were quite a few unread messages but the one at the top of the list was from Brenda. He deleted it from the inbox, went into the trash and deleted it permanently, and then logged out. He turned toward her. "There. You see? No problem at all." He walked over and plopped himself down on the couch beside her. He put his hand on her knee but she was unwilling to show him any signs of loosening up.

"What's on your mind?"

"Explain to me again how this is all going to work?"

"I'll go into the office tomorrow and...."

"No, silly. I get that, I'm talking about the deal. I'm still not sure how this is going to all work out in our favor."

"Ah, I see. How far back do you want me to go? How much detail do you want?" He put his arm around her and gave her a kiss on the cheek.

"Start at the beginning, make it a high level summary, and don't use fancy business words."

"Right, okay. So my sister's husband had this good idea, only it wasn't that good an idea. Just okay, but great potential. Think of it like the Rubik's Cube. If back in the eighties someone would have asked for investments, people would have laughed them out of the room. Well, my brother-in-law's idea is kind of like that. He did a ton of research and found a potential investor in Russia, but there was just one trick. They didn't want to start cranking out a gazillion of these things. They wanted to do a trial balloon."

"Trial balloon?"

"Yeah, if he could show them orders for some they would get on board for a boatload more. I mean a lot more. This is where I come in. I went and did some digging of my own and, thanks to you and your wonderful knowledge of your husband's business, I found someone who liked the idea and would sign on for a decent-sized order, provided the price wasn't too high."

"So, he's not a totally useless jerk."

"Let's not get carried away. Your husband would put in some cash but probably make a fair bit of money in a matter of days. Plus, the idea isn't that great so he'd see no long term benefit—or any desire to pursue it further since it's not one of his core businesses. My brother-in-law will basically make his money back plus a little for his trouble and your narcissistic prick of a husband will be happy and call it a day."

"That sounds more like Thomas."

"Once that deal is done, the Russian investor comes in and backs a dump truck of money up to the door. My brother-in-law and I, since I'm in for half of the investment, make out like bandits, and I share it with you after you divorce the son-of-a-bitch and get half of everything."

"We have a prenup, but I'm less worried because as long as he doesn't know about us, he's the cheater and I have proof. Anyway, I'm not so sure there's much of anything to get half of. He's an idiot, but I'm also sure he's good at making us look rich without actually being rich." She put her hand on top of his. "Will this really work?"

"It already has, my dear. The ink is dry on the contract. Thomas saw a few nice numbers on the horizon and signed the deal. On Monday the initial investor will sign on and this stupid do-dad will be in every department store that's not Walmart in the United States."

"Why not Walmart?"

Anthony smiled. "Because that's who my Russian guy sells to. Plus, he sells to Canada, Australia, most of Europe and who the hell knows where else. He also sells to Michael's and is going to get it onto Amazon. This thing is going to be under every damn Christmas tree and on every wish list for every kid whose family has more than two nickels to rub together. Remember *Tickle Me Elmo?*"

Brenda nodded.

"Well this thing is going to make sales of that thing look like nothing. And again, it's not even that good a thing."

"Then how is it going to be so popular, exactly?"

Anthony smiled again. "Because some rich Russian guy is going to tell them it is. Grownups are stupid and kids don't know how the world works yet. No one likes to think for themselves. If there's one thing that works on them it's propaganda and the Russians are pros at it."

Brenda leaned over and gave Anthony a kiss on the cheek. He turned his head and tried to plant a kiss on her lips. She blocked him by putting her hand in front of her mouth. "Not until you go and delete that email from the office computer. Then, I'll give you some sugar and you can see what I sent you in that email for real."

"It's going to take at least twenty minutes each way."

"I won't go anywhere, I promise. Oh, well—I might move from here into the bedroom."

Anthony grabbed his keys off this desk and headed out the front door.

SATURDAY, JULY 8, 1:00 P.M.

Anthony made it to the office in record time. He checked the fax machine, and there was nothing there. He walked over to his desk and there was nothing in his tray that his office assistant would have left on his desk. He sat down and wheeled his chair over to the office assistant's computer and logged in. He opened the email, deleted Brenda's message, and then shut down the computer. He walked around the office looking for anything that faxed, or emailed, and printed. His office consisted of a single trailer with three small desks, three phones, a printer, a fax machine, a water cooler, a microwave, and a two-piece bathroom in one corner. It didn't take him long to exhaust his search. He opened his flip phone and held down the number five to speed dial his brother-in-law, who picked up on the first ring.

"Yeah, hey, Stephen, it's Anthony. Why don't I have any papers from Thomas yet?"

"You don't have them? Shit. His secretary was supposed to make copies and then send over mine."

"Are you telling me Thomas is the only one with a copy of the contract?"

"A signed one with all the last minute changes, yeah."

"Shit. Wait, what do you mean 'last minute changes'?"

"I realized that I could squeeze a bit, so I squeezed a bit."

"Shit, Stephen, we talked about this. We take whatever deal he puts on the table, remember?"

"Relax, it's okay. He signed it and left for the day to go visit his mistress or girlfriend or whoever. I saw his secretary walk out of the room with the only signed copy. It's probably sitting on her desk copied and ready to go. You should have it first thing Monday morning."

"So long as you're sure. Why would you try to squeeze more? There's a lot more coming, you know."

"I couldn't resist. He's such a colossal dill-hole I had to squeeze as much as I could out of him. He thinks he's onto a bit of easy money but doesn't have a clue. With our little side payment to his manufacturer, he's going to have to eat so much cost to meet his end of the deal that he'll be lucky if he makes half of what he thought he would."

"He's going to be pissed."

"I don't care. I'll get back enough to fix the hole in my roof and you'll make enough for an upgrade to your trailer, but that's hardly the point. We're basically getting licensing fees for doing very little. Thomas makes a pittance, I—*WE*—make out like bandits after our Russian friend saturates the market with something no one needs but must have at all costs. Everybody wins."

"Everyone who matters, wins."

Stephen let out a chuckle. "Now you're starting to sound like him."

Anthony didn't chuckle. "Asshole. Look, just call his secretary first thing Monday morning and get her to send the contract over, okay? Once I have it in hand I'll feel much better."

CHAPTER*THREE*

When Brenda came home from her night out at the girls, she stepped on something the second she closed the door, and it just about sent her careening into the umbrella stand. At first she figured it was the martinis she had while out with the girls, but then she saw the small green lime go shooting across the foyer tile.

"Ugh!" Her blood pressure rose with each step that brought her closer to the living room. There were piles of half-eaten nachos on the table with only a few of them actually left on the plate. None were on the now-ruined baking sheet sitting askew on the coffee table. Candy bar wrappers littered the couch and, by her quick count, *eleven* empty beer bottles strewn across the floor. She picked up a throw pillow that appeared clean on both sides, likely tossed overboard before things got too messy, and stared at it. "I'm married to a disgusting pig."

A quick walkabout confirmed nothing was broken, and then she got a glimpse of the kitchen. It was so bad she didn't need to step any closer to come to the conclusion that she was going to spend the night in the spare bedroom. Wandering down the hall, she shuffled her feet and tried to not let the latest realization of being married to someone she loathed kill her buzz from an otherwise wonderful evening out with a few of her girlfriends.

Peeking into her mother-in-law's room confirmed that she was sleeping peacefully and walking past Brittany's open door confirmed her daughter was still at a friend's place waiting for the argument she had with her father to blow over. She slid into one of the apartment's three sparsely decorated but otherwise quiet and comfortable extra bedrooms and shut the door behind her. It wasn't until she kicked off her shoes and stripped down to her bra and underpants that she realized she didn't have any of her sleeping clothes, or even a t-shirt. She shrugged her shoulders, tossed her bra onto the pile of clothes on the floor beside her shoes, and crawled into the luxurious king-sized bed.

SUNDAY, JULY 9, 6:00 P.M.

In an effort to avoid Thomas as much as possible that day, Brenda slept in as long as she could. By eleven o'clock she found it impossible to sleep any longer. With the exception of a brief, and not entirely cordial, exchange of words with him after yoga she managed to avoid all contact with him until dinner time. She should have known the smell of food would bring him out of his cave, but she was hungry and in the mood to cook a meal. After another short battle of words with her husband before dinner, she watched him walk toward his office with his plate of food. She hoped this would lead to a long bout of the silent treatment but wasn't about to hold her breath.

Appetite ruined, she flopped herself down on the couch and turned on the TV. Staring down at her phone, she picked it up and glanced over her shoulder to see if there was any movement from down the hall. Convinced the coast was clear she picked up her phone and sent a text to Anthony.

B: *Hey there, big boy.*

Within a few seconds, his reply came through.

A: *Well isn't this a nice surprise. To what do I owe the pleasure?*

B: *He's sulking in his office. I'm considering watching shows.*

A: *Up for a little Netflix and chill, eh?*

She pondered his request for a moment. There was no way she could be quiet or discreet enough to be able to pull that off with Thomas in the house, regardless of how far she let it go.

B: *Are you crazy? He's just down the hall in his office!*

A: *Live a little. I'm sitting on the couch all alone thinking of you.*

B: *Well that's just it. I'm not alone!*

A: *If I was home with you I wouldn't hide out in my office ignoring you.*

B: *That's sweet of you to say.*

A: *I'd be with you.*

B: *Oh, really?*

A: *Really, really. It's just too bad you're not in bed.*

B: *Oh?*

A: *That way I could crawl into bed with you, let the full weight of my body gently fall on top of you, brush any stray strands of hair away from your face, look you in the eyes, tell you how much I love you, and kiss you.*

B: *Oh, my! I love you, too, handsome.*

A: *I dream about lying with you in a soft, warm bed and feeling your body against mine as our tongues dance and our hands explore. The feeling of your body heat mixed with mine. The taste of your mouth mixed with mine. Legs intertwined. The look in your eyes every time our kiss breaks and our souls merge.*

She got up from the couch and made her way into the bedroom where she lay down on her back on her side of the bed. She enabled the selfie camera on her phone and took a picture. The light made it look like she was just a head floating in space, but it would have to do. She sent it to him with a brief message.

B: *Go on.*

A: *I pull you in close to me so there's almost no space between us. I whisper, "I love you" into your ear and before you can respond I add, "Your disembodied head can tell the rest of you later." You let out a giggle, the sound of which fills my heart with joy, and I can feel your body vibrating against mine as you attempt to stifle your laughter. I reach down and give your bum a solid pinch and instantaneously a giggle turns into a squeal and you put your hands on my cheeks and you kiss me, gently at first, and then deeper and deeper with each breath.*

B: *Oh, Anthony!*

A: *I roll you over so you're on top of me and sit you up, a leg on either side of my hips, your full weight, or almost, on top of me. Joined but not joined. I put my hands on your hips as I wiggle mine. You lean your head down and your long, black hair falls off your shoulders creating a curtain around my face. You lean down and put your lips against mine, open your mouth, and give me your tongue. I slowly take it into my mouth and suck on it. Your body rocks back and forth as my hands massage your hips and backside.*

B: *Your words, Anthony. Where did you learn to write such beautiful things?*

A: *It's easy when the object of my affection is so radiant and so beautiful.*

B: **blush**

A; *I release your tongue and the tips touch. You smile and shoot me a devilish glance as you reposition your hips. My eyes widen at the sensation and you take my tongue into your mouth. My head rests on the pillow and my hands slide up and down your sides. Our bodies rock up and down and back and forth together. My fingertips glide across your smooth skin, exploring all your curves.*

B: *I like it when you do that.*

A: *You release my tongue and we share a deep, passionate kiss. Our lips part and I sneak a nibble of your lower lip as my hips push and lift you off the bed, my hands on your sides to steady you. You let out a gasp bordering on a squeal as I let you down quickly, your torso falling onto mine, the warmth of your skin against mine as you nuzzle your face into my neck and kiss it.*

B: *Have you shaved?*

A; *No, ma'am. I know you dig the beard.*

B: *Mmm.*

A: *I roll you over so you can feel the weight of me again and we exchange more passionate kisses as I press myself against you and thrust my hips. You can feel the texture of my hair against your smooth skin as you give yourself to me. I lean up and put my hands onto your shoulders and look you in the eyes as I rock you back and forth, your mouth held open as you let out small gasps of air with every one of my movements.*

B: *Oh, Anthony. Please, more!*

A: *I lay my chest down on top of you and your arms wrap around my back and your legs around my hips. I bite your lower lip again, this time with more emphasis and your breathing becomes heavier. I can feel your fingernails start to dig into my back and I thrust with more force and increased frequency. Gasps of air become moans and your legs tighten around me and your nails break the skin of my back.*

B: Yes! Keep going. I'm almost there.

A: I thrust harder and faster and your moans become louder. Your hips push back against mine as you feel it building. Your entire body aches for release. You call out my name as all the muscles in your body contract. Time freezes momentarily.

B: OMG. Yes yes yes!

A: After two beats of our hearts waves of pleasure erupt and our sweat-covered bodies twist and contort with each other. Falling down on top of you we can each feel the other's heart pounding, our chests rising and falling with deep breaths.

B: Mmmm, Anthony, that was fantastic.

A: I wipe your brow with my hand and kiss your forehead, then your nose, then your lips, holding mine against yours. I look into your eyes and I can see right to your heart. We say, "I love you" and then "jinx" at the same time and you giggle. It's the last sound made before we fall asleep in each other's arms.

B: You're so good with words.

A: Thank you. What's your plan now? Any chance you can find an excuse to get out of the house.

B: Now, I lay here and bask in my satisfied glow for a bit then I get back to the couch and Netflix. I might read for a bit before bed.

A: Sounds good, my sweet. Text me to say goodnight.

B: I will.

A: I love you.

B: I love you, too.

She lay in bed for a few minutes with her eyes closed before rolling off the side, standing up, and straightening her clothes. She walked down the hall to the living room and poked her head around the corner of the hallway leading to Thomas's office, his door still shut. She settled on the couch to watch The Notebook and managed to watch a good ninety minutes of the film uninterrupted before hearing his office door fly open and his clumsy footsteps lumber into the kitchen. She concentrated on the movie as he yanked open the fridge door and clanked around the glassware, slammed one down on the counter, and poured himself something to drink.

He walked into the living room and stood in silence for a few seconds before speaking. "Whatcha watching?"

"*The Notebook.*"

"Who's in it?"

"Ryan Gosling and Rachel McAdams. Shh. It's almost over."

"Sappy love story? Let me guess, they fall in love, face challenges and doubt, kiss, and live happily ever after."

She shifted her position on the couch and ignored him, focusing instead on the film.

"Well, am I right?"

She reached forward for the remote and turned up the volume. She raised her arm over the back of the couch and with her other hand she extended a middle finger. Her eyes never left the television.

He shuffled back into the kitchen mumbling and with a loud whack slammed his glass down on the counter and headed down the hallway towards his mother's room.

SUNDAY, JULY 9, 11:00 P.M.

After watching a couple of shows on Netflix, Brenda realized that Thomas hadn't come out of his mother's room in a couple hours. She got up and walked over to the room and peeked in through the door. He was asleep in the chair, slumped over, with his face resting on the edge of the bed and his hardcover copy of *A Tale of Two Cities* on the floor. She shut the door and walked back into the living room and grabbed her cell phone out of her purse. She made her way to the bedroom and packed an overnight bag and, keeping her voice low, called Anthony.

"*Hey sweetness, why are you calling? Is everything all right?*"

"Yeah. Yeah. Thanks for asking. Thomas fell asleep reading to his mother. I'm coming over to spend the night, if that's alright."

"*If that's all right? Of course it's all right. Did you guys have a fight? Won't he wonder where you are? Will you leave a note for him? Won't he be worried? Won't he be pissed?*"

"I'll answer in the order you asked them. No, we didn't have a fight. Yes, he will wonder where I am. No, I won't be leaving him a note. He doesn't worry about anyone but himself. I hope he's angrier than he's ever been." She tiptoed barefoot out of the apartment carrying her shoes in one hand and her gym bag over her shoulder. "Okay, I'm getting in the elevator. I'm told the damn thing acts like a Fahrenheit cage so I'll probably lose you."

"I think you mean Faraday cage."

"What?"

"You said, Fahrenheit cage. I think you meant Faraday cage. It's a device that is impervious to magnetic fields."

"If it makes your phone not work then that's the thing."

"I'm sure there's not any need for one of those in your building, not unless there are giant magnets all over the place. You probably just get dodgy reception because it's an elevator in the centre of a brick and steel building and surrounded by all kinds of other interference. I'll see you in a few. Drive safe."

Brenda hopped into the elevator and checked her cell signal. No bars. "Stupid elevator."

She arrived at Anthony's house in half an hour, pleased with her time despite the bridge traffic. She killed the ignition and checked her phone and ensured there was nothing waiting from Thomas or Brittany. She stepped out of the car and reached back in to grab her overnight bag. The house was dark save one light in the living room and there were no signs of life anywhere. She walked into the house quietly, mindful of the fact that Anthony may have fallen asleep in his chair waiting for her. Sleep was wonderful. With the exception of Thomas, she felt bad whenever she woke someone up.

He sat in the living room in a big chair with a bottle of Lot no. 40 Canadian whisky on the table and a glass in his hand half filled with the light brown elixir and a few cubes of ice. His laptop rested on his thighs and cast an eerie glow on his face in contrast with the small table lamp beside him. It made Brenda think she should put on some old school red-and-blue 3D glasses. He was staring at the screen reading an email and didn't look up from the computer but greeted her with a smile nonetheless.

"Hey sweetheart, how was the drive?"

Brenda walked over, stood beside his chair, and put her hand on the back of his neck. She gave it a gentle rub. "A bit of traffic for some reason, but it wasn't too bad. Why are you just sitting there reading an email with a drink beside you that has too much ice in it?"

"I like my drinks really cold."

"But the ice waters down the flavor."

"I usually drink 'em too fast for that to be a problem."

"And what has captured all your attention on your computer?"

"An email from Stephen outlining the changes he made to the contract."

She stood up and looked down at the screen in his lap. "Oh? Thomas didn't say anything to me when he got home. Not that he would, but still…."

"Well that's just the thing. He apparently signed and it was all good, but until I have the papers in my hand it's not a done deal. He's going to call Thomas's secretary first thing in the morning."

Brenda took the drink from his hand and had a sip. "Hmm."

"Hmm?"

"You're not drinking this fast enough. Your ice is melting and the balance is all off. Also, my husband is going to wake up and positively freak out that no one is home. The last thing he's going to do is think about work and some contract that he already thinks has been sent over."

Anthony took his drink back and poured a bit more whisky. "But that's the thing, it wasn't sent over. I'm worried."

Brenda unzipped the back of her skirt and let it fall to the floor revealing a pair of silk high cut underwear. "Why don't you leave the questions and the laptop and worry about something else for a few minutes?"

CHAPTER*FOUR*

MONDAY, JULY 10, 9:00 A.M.

She opened her eyes and smelled bacon. She put her hand out beside her only to find empty sheets. It took her a few seconds to orient herself after waking in a strange bed, but once she did she smiled and reflected on an evening of passionate love making with Anthony. He needed a distraction and she had provided several. She got out of bed and wandered downstairs in her camisole. He was standing in the kitchen in a bathrobe with a spatula and a frying pan of sizzling bacon and eggs. He turned to see a nearly naked Brenda standing in the doorway.

"Well, hello, nurse. I wish I could have that vision of beauty standing in front of me every morning."

"Well, you will soon enough I suppose, and who knows? Maybe if Thomas doesn't completely lose his shit over this little overnight I can make up some more excuses to spend the night more often."

Anthony walked over to the kitchen table with a plate of bacon and eggs and stopped by the toaster to pick up a couple of pieces of whole wheat toast. "Now, that is something that pleases me. Here. Sit. Eat some breakfast." He took off his robe to reveal a pair of blue silk pyjamas. He wrapped her in the robe and tied the front, kissing her on the nose.

"You don't want to watch me eat my breakfast practically nude?"

Anthony's eyebrows raised and his eyes widened. *"Au contraire.* I could stare at your beauty all day. If I were an artist surely you'd be my muse. As it stands though, all that food is really hot and I shudder at the thought of you scorching any of your delicate lady bits on my watch."

"You'd have to kiss them better."

Anthony cleared his throat. "That may very well be true, but I'd rather not take the chance. Sit. Eat." Anthony brought his plate over and joined Brenda at the table. "So, thanks for getting my mind off of everything last night."

"Oh, it was my pleasure."

"Anyway, I called Stephen first thing this morning and reminded him to call your husband's office to rattle the cage."

Brenda looked up from her meal. "I don't know what time his little slut secretary gets into the office, but I think the little whore has the messages go to her voicemail."

"Jeepers, Brenda, you really don't like his secretary. You know you should let go of some of that anger."

Brenda waggled a slice of bacon at him. "You just shut your pie hole, mister. I'm pretty sure she's sleeping with him. She knows he's married and she knows he's got a mistress. That means she's just doing him for a nice Christmas bonus and a better than average increase in pay every April. That makes her a whore."

"Infallible logic. How long have you known about the mistress? Who is she?"

"I don't know who she is. Some young tart named Trixie or Nikki or something like that. People talk. Especially when your husband is a total dick to just about everyone he meets."

"He really is."

"He doesn't have too many friends who will protect his secrets. I've suspected it was happening for a while and I've known for sure for about a year and a half."

"You started seeing me about a year ago."

"Yeah, I did. You worried I'm just using you to get back at him?"

Anthony shook his head. "I know you are to a certain degree, but I also know you wouldn't keep coming back if you didn't genuinely like me, so I'm not worried."

"That's sweet of you to say, and it's true."

The rest of the breakfast proceeded in silence and when both plates were empty Anthony stood and grabbed Brenda's plate off the table before she had the chance to take it away herself.

"I'll clean up, you go shower and I'll meet you in there in a few minutes." He gave her a nod and a wink.

Brenda stood and dropped his bathrobe to the ground. As she walked away she turned her head back toward him. He was stealing a solid look at her backside. In his bedroom she removed her camisole and stood naked checking her phone. She had one message and wasn't the least bit surprised that it was Thomas completely freaking out about where she was and decided against calling him back. He needed to suffer. Making her way to the washroom where she brushed her teeth and hopped in the luxurious shower she paid careful attention to the craftsmanship of the building. She had always imagined that a contractor construction guy would have half-finished projects all over the place, her theory being he would always be so busy doing everyone else's jobs that his own would never bubble up to the top of the list. While that may be true for some guys, Anthony was the owner of an extremely large operation and did very little hands-on construction work anymore. He still had the burning desire to build and create, so his own house looked like a well-crafted palace.

He joined her in the shower as she was rinsing her hair, and stepping into the middle of the multi-streamed arrangement of shower heads and jets scattered along three of the four walls. They had passionate stand-up sex and took full advantage of several of the removable shower wand's stream settings. Brenda got dressed and put on her watch.

"Shouldn't you be at work?"

"Nah, my brother has it covered today. I'll make it up to him by getting him out of the house for a poker game or something one night when his battle-axe wife is giving him grief over something."

Brenda cackled then covered her mouth. "I'm sorry, that was mean. It's just that it sounds like we should get her together with my husband."

"They'd make quite the pair. Perfect for parties and family events."

"No doubt. Hey, I should get back home. If he catches me cheating I don't get anything in the divorce. Stupid prenup. If I get caught doing this —" she put her hand between Anthony's legs and gave him a gentle squeeze—"I'm cut off."

His eyebrows rose. "Spectacular imagery." He moved her hand away from his crotch. "What time is it, anyway?"

"Just after eleven. With the city traffic being what it is I don't expect to get home until noon."

"Good luck."

MONDAY, JULY 10, 12:00 P.M.

Jenny ran down the hallway to the office, keys in one hand, and several shopping bags in the other. Whenever Thomas was not at work she took advantage of the free time and went shopping. She checked the messages first thing before heading to the office, got his message about not coming in, and went out for a little retail therapy, completely forgetting the request from Stephen to fax the contract back as soon as possible. In spite of all the perks she gave Thomas, she was sure he would fire her if she forgot to do it. There was already one call from him in the calls log on her phone. She dropped her shopping bags inside the door and headed straight to her desk, where the contract sat copied but otherwise untouched from Friday afternoon. She faxed the paperwork to the number Stephen had given her and then called his cell phone.

"Hello?" he said.

"Hi, it's Jenny from Thomas Van Steen's office. I just want to confirm a fax came through."

"I'm not near my fax machine right now but I'll call over to see that it came through."

"Perfect, thank you."

*CHAPTER*FIVE

Thomas looked at his watch. Twenty minutes had passed since the power went out and five since he found out that his wife was not simply in bed, but also conspiring with their contractor who was in cahoots with science-nerd Stephen. He was sure he plugged his mother back into the right socket but in his mind he just couldn't see the plug sticking out of the orange-edged outlet. He looked at the doors to the elevator and decided he had no other option.

He wedged his fingers between the elevator doors and pulled at the doors from the middle. They didn't budge. Managing to get both sets of fingers in the small gap between the doors, he realized he needed more leverage. With one foot on the floor, he braced himself and got the other leg up on the wall above the handrail. His arms pulled and his leg pushed and he was finally to get the doors open enough to see through.

The top foot of the elevator door showed the bottom of the doors from the hallway. He was too far down to escape from inside.

He needed to get on top.

He caught his breath and looked at the monitor. Mitch was still dancing around like a fool but he saw a shadow coming in through the door. His heart skipped a beat and when they came into view his eyes widened and rage took over. It was Nikki. He got closer to the speaker so he could try to make out the conversation over the music playing. Mitch looked as surprised as Thomas was angry.

"Jewell, what the fuck? Are you crazy?"

Thomas's mind was racing. "Jewell?"

Nikki took Mitch by the arm and walked him around to the back of the security desk. She turned down the speakers. "There. Now we can hear if anyone is coming."

"Honey, this is insane. If he catches you here you are royally screwed. If he catches you here with me, we're both screwed. Everything we've been working for will go right down the toilet."

"Relax, Mitchie." Nikki put her hand on his shoulder and with the other hand dug into her purse. She pulled out a bundle of hundred dollar bills and plopped it down on the desk.

"Jesus Christ. Where the hell did you get that?" He looked down at his desk calendar. "It's not allowance time."

"Thomas. He basically paid me to screw him on a stack of money at the bank. I figure this should cover the next few poker games?"

"And then some, yeah. He whooped me the other night."

"Don't sound so down. I've been keeping us flush with cash since I hooked up with the clueless old fart."

"I know it's his money, but I don't like losing." He picked up the stack of bills and thumbed through it. "Jesus, that's a lot of Benjamins. I have a question. How big a stack of money?"

"It didn't look like much, you know? I thought that kind of cash would look more… impressive."

"How much?"

"One-point-eight million."

Mitch sat down in his chair and rubbed his hands through his hair. "Jesus. You had sex on top of one-point-eight million dollars cash?"

"Yep, and I think I know how I can get it."

She sat down on his lap and ground her butt into his crotch. Mitch stopped her and looked her in the eye. "How exactly do you plan on doing that? I thought we were playing the long-haul grift here. Why get greedy now?"

She gave him a kiss on the tip of his nose. "Because we can, and because it will be just that damn easy."

Thomas stared at the monitor, fists clenched and knuckles white, with blood clotting on the ones on his right hand from his earlier fit of rage. "You bitch." He hammered his hand against the call button and yelled again. "You fucking bitch. You're not getting a goddamn cent of it, you fucking whore." Thomas slammed his fist against the monitor and the glass spider webbed like the one below it. A few shards fell to the ground and fresh blood trickled across his hand. The image on the monitor fragmented, pulsed, and wobbled as Thomas slid to the floor.

*PART*TWO

NIKKI & MITCH

*CHAPTER*SIX

FRIDAY, JULY 7, 3:00 P.M.

After the adrenaline rush from his encounter at the gym, Thomas's heart was racing. He wiped a bead of sweat off his forehead with his sleeve and made his way across town to Nikki's. He was in no mood to test his heart with more excitement, so he followed the speed limit and kept both hands on the wheel. He pulled in front of her building and paranoia got the better of him so he avoided a parking spot right near the entrance and opted to take something a little less conspicuous around the corner.

The air was humid and stale and had an odor he couldn't quite place. He checked his breath by blowing into his cupped hand and rang the buzzer. Looking around to make sure he didn't notice anyone or anything out of the ordinary, he pressed the buzzer a second time and shifted his weight from foot to foot.

"Hello?"

"Hey babe, it's me."

"Thomas! You're earlier than I thought you'd be. I look like crap."

"Well, don't do your hair just yet. I need time to mess it up. Now let me in before someone sees me standing out here like some kind of loser."

The door buzzed and he heard the familiar click of the latch unlocking. He opened the door and decided to take the stairs. It was only one flight up and there were always fewer people in the stairs. Apartment 201 was one of the larger units and he made sure it was the nicest one on the floor. He would have sprung for a penthouse but Nikki was not fond of heights. There were always too many freaks and crackheads wandering around and up to no good, so for safety reasons a ground floor apartment was out of the question. He poked his head out of the stairwell and gave a look down the end of the long hallway. Satisfied the coast was clear he knocked. Showing his trademarked lack of patience he waited no more than two seconds before letting himself into the apartment. The smell of Nikki's coconut oil hair and body products smacked him in the face. Nikki was in the bathroom frantically trying to make herself presentable.

"Hey, babe. I said don't worry about it. Geez, why are you always so concerned with looking pretty for me? Look pretty for everyone else. I just need you naked."

Nikki leaned her head back so she could see through the doorway. "Are you saying I'm not pretty?"

"No. I mean, yes, you're pretty. You're stunning. You just don't have to do anything extra for me. I love you natural."

"Natural, huh?" Nikki stepped back and lifted up her towel to expose a perfectly smooth pubic region. "Would you like this to be all natural? Because last time I checked you preferred smooth."

Thomas licked his lips and threw his gym bag down on the floor beside the couch. He walked toward the bathroom but didn't go in. Instead, he reached inside. He lifted the back of her towel and stole a glance at her bum. She swatted his hand away. "Mind your manners, mister. I'll let you know when I'm ready for playtime."

"You just lifted your towel to show me your pussy and I can't sneak a peek at your ass while I'm waiting?"

"First of all, you know I'm not a fan of that word. Second, you can't just go looking up skirts. Maybe you can get away with that with your wife or that tart at the office but you can't just take what you want from me. You have to earn it." She tapped him on the nose with the tip of her finger and then gave him a wink before returning to her eyeliner.

"If you weren't so damn beautiful...."

"Yeah, but I am that damn beautiful, and you love me. Now, go into the bedroom and light some candles and lose your shirt and pants while I finish my makeup. Red lipstick today?"

Thomas made his way to the bedroom. "Yes, please. I'm in a red lipstick kind of mood." He lit all the candles he could find in the room, shut the blinds, and turned out the lights. He had to admit, it looked downright romantic. Romance at home stopped more than a decade ago. He undressed and toiled with the question of whether or not to leave his boxer shorts on. Nikki was amazing in the sack, but she didn't like crass, and lying naked on the bed with a raging hard-on as she walked in the room seemed a bit crass. Then again, any time he left his boxers on, removing them was the first thing she did. He took off his boxers and slid under the sheets and felt that that was an acceptable compromise. He reached for the remote control for the stereo, found a classical station, and lowered the volume down to a more acceptable level. He figured she must have been driving her neighbors crazy with all the loud music she normally blared.

Nikki slid into the bedroom with all the grace and elegance of a Golden Age Hollywood star. She gave him a nod and a pretend curtsey in appreciation of how he had prepared the room. She slid under the covers and caught a peek and rolled her eyes. "You know I don't like it when you're just all out there like that. Put your boxer shorts back on."

"But—but—but the first thing you do is take them off."

Nikki folded her arms and let out a huff. "It is not the first thing I do and you know it. I like to cuddle and kiss first. Then, you go down on me, because I like the way your mouth warms me up. Then, you take off my nightie or my t-shirt or whatever I'm wearing. Then, then I take off your boxer shorts. It's like the fourth or fifth thing that happens, which is nowhere close to the first thing. Now put them back on and stop pointing that thing at me for a few minutes."

"But they're just going to come back off."

"Only if you're lucky. And don't be such a suck, it's very unbecoming."

Thomas exhaled deeply and grabbed his boxer shorts from the ground and slid them back on. "There."

"Much better. Now kiss me."

Thomas having sex with Nikki wasn't what he would call risky, or even that adventurous, but it was always enjoyable. She reaped the rewards of having a sugar daddy nearly twice her age and he—well, he got to sleep with a gorgeous woman twenty years his junior. Cuddling before and after was mandatory.

—

Nikki lay back in bed, fully satisfied, and flipped the radio station off of classical. Neil Diamond's "Sweet Caroline" played and she turned up the volume. "Oh, I love this song!" She lit up a cigarette and offered Thomas a drag. He took a long pull and attempted but failed to blow a smoke circle.

"It's good to see that my taste in music is finally starting to rub off on you."

Nikki took another drag and blew a perfect circle in his direction. "I love The Diamond. Always have. He's one of my favorite old singers."

"It pains me that there wasn't even a hint of sarcasm in your voice just now."

Nikki gave him a wink and took another drag and instead of another smoke circle she exhaled into his face and pulled all the covers to the side. "You're old, but not as old as Neil Diamond. Get over yourself. I'm cold."

Thomas got up and made his way to the shower. "Did you pick up more of that unscented soap I told you to get?"

"It's under the sink beside my tampons."

"Of course it is." Thomas mumbled as he opened the cupboard under the sink and rummaged around. He found the soap between a box of tampons and a tube of Colgate toothpaste. "Hey, did you get different toothpaste?"

"I thought I'd like the taste better than the other kind. I was wrong. You want it for your gym bag?"

"Nah, I'm a Crest guy." Thomas showered and returned to Nikki's bedroom to put his clothes on. She was snuggled under the covers with just her eyes visible from under the duvet.

"When are you going to leave her?"

He sat down on the end of the bed. "We've been over this. When Brittany is out of the house, and when I no longer have to look after my mother. You knew this from the start. I've been completely transparent. Is what I provide not enough? You know, it's more than most women ever get. You know that, right?"

Nikki put her hand on his shoulder. "No, no, no, sweetie. You're right. It's just that I want you all the time, and all to myself."

"Hey, you've come a long way since your days at the gym."

"That was the best job I ever had."

"Working the front counter at a smelly gym?"

"Yeah, if I wouldn't have gotten that job I wouldn't have met you."

Thomas kissed her forehead. "Just give it some more time. Speaking of which, I gotta get going. The old ball-and-chain is dragging me out to some fucking fundraiser tonight."

"*Old* ball-and-chain? I thought she was younger than you."

Thomas dressed without further comment and made his way back to his car.

FRIDAY, JULY 7, 5:55 P.M.

Thomas walked up the stairs from the parking garage and stopped in the lobby to pick up the mail. On the way back from the mailbox the doorman caught his attention. He always thought Mitch was one step removed from being a frat boy, too dumb or lazy to make it onto the police force, so now he sat on his ass all day, watching Thomas's building and reading up on poker. That was one thing he had a knack for—his one redeemable skill—playing poker. He was even responsible for getting Thomas into a regular game, although he hadn't been able to reconcile how he managed to afford the thousand dollar buy-in. "Hey Mitch, saving the building from crazed pizza delivery men one day at a time?"

"Good evening, Mr. Van Steen. I was wondering if you would like to partake in a friendly card game later this evening."

"Shit, I'd love to, but I have this stupid fundraiser to go to with the missus. Besides, aren't you tired of me taking all your money?"

Mitch picked up a small leather-bound notebook from the desk and flipped through it. "It would appear you're on a bit of a run as of late but I'm not too worried about it."

Thomas wasn't sure who was bankrolling the kid. He sat on the building management board and knew exactly what his salary was. Unless he was living out of the YMCA and eating instant noodles twice a day there was no way he would be playing in any of these games. They were decidedly above his pay grade. "Tell you what, Mitchy boy. I'll make up some excuse to get out of this thing. You count me in. Who all will be there? The usual group of suckers?"

"Yeah, plus a couple new ones. Friends of mine I don't mind stealing from. It'll come down to two of you and me and Sid, I'm sure."

Thomas tapped the security desk with his stack of mail. "Right then, same place?"

"Yes, sir."

Thomas headed into the elevator and swiped his key fob and entered his PIN on the numeric keypad before pressing "P." Three monitors adorned the high-tech elevator panel. The building management board received some complaints from the older occupants about safety, and in response they sprung for the most technologically-advanced building security they could find, and this included the elevator. The top monitor showed live views from each level of the East stairwell. Pressing a button beside the monitor activated the microphone attached to that camera so those in the elevator could hear. The middle monitor worked in the exact same way but for the West stairwell. The bottom monitor displayed a view of the floor they were approaching as well as a toggle button to cycle through the floors and the lobby. This screen had two buttons—one activated the audio and the other a microphone that allowed for two-way communication. All monitors had a keypad beside them that allowed for someone to press a button corresponding to a floor, and the camera feed would switch to show that location.

He never paid attention to any floor other than the penthouse. He always pressed "P" for all three monitors and enabled the audio. He wasn't paranoid, not about someone robbing him at least, but he suspected his wife was cheating on him and was always on the lookout for someone sneaking out of the top floor or having what was supposed to be a private conversation on their cell phone. His paranoia didn't pay any dividends for this particular journey.

FRIDAY, JULY 7, 9:30 P.M.

Thomas hailed a cab and gave the driver the address of the poker game. He pulled a pack of cigarettes out of his jacket pocket and lit one up without asking. The cab driver rolled down both rear windows and said, "No, please, do whatever you want. You're the customer. Smoke in my car all you want." Without looking up from his smart phone he gave the cabbie the finger. Half a block short of the destination the cab pulled over and the driver yelled back to him, "Get out here."

"But the address is up there."

"I need to turn around. Easier to do here. That'll be seventeen-fifty."

Thomas fished a twenty out of his wallet and then thought better of it and handed the cabbie a ten, a five and three singles. He butted his cigarette out on the floor of the cab before exiting. The cab started to turn around just as he swung the door shut and almost nudged him with the rear bumper. The car peeled away and the cab driver shot his arm out the window and extended his middle finger as it tore off down the street. "Asshole." He started to walk toward his destination. They played every game at the same house, and he wasn't sure why. The set-up was okay, nothing fancy, and the game was low stakes compared to some of the other illegal operations. It consisted of a fairly consistent group of guys and one girl—the host, Sidney. At first he wasn't that keen on playing poker with a woman, but over time she showed him she was more like a dude than most of the other players so he tolerated her presence.

The buy-in was one thousand dollars and the pot was winner take all, minus five hundred bucks for expenses like food and alcohol and cab rides home for people who'd had too much to drink. Any left over from the five hundred went into a "Poker Game Improvement Fund" which paid for cards when decks wore out and repairs to the tables. Once in a while on special occasions they would take some money out of the improvement fund and have dealers come in, though he made sure they were always attractive women. No one ever complained.

He knocked on the door and lit up a cigarette and thought about pitching it to the ground out of disgust but decided he would rather smoke it instead. The curtains to the right of the door moved as someone peeked through the window, and then the door opened. With the cigarette in a precarious dangle hung from his lip, he wasted no time getting right to the insults. "I'm here for amateur hour poker hosted by a humorless twatwaffle."

"Smoke my ass hair, Thomas, but smoke it outside. I don't want you making my place smell any worse than you already do. Same goes for that nasty cancer stick."

Thomas butted out the cigarette on the front stoop and walked into the townhome. There were two tables set up, one in the kitchen and one in the sitting area. There were chips for eight players at each table. Thomas spotted Mitch at one of the tables and gave him a nod as he approached. "Looks like we got what? Sixteen people here tonight?" Thomas directed the question at Mitch but a guy he didn't recognize answered.

"Yep. It's gonna be epic."

He raised his eyebrows and looked over at his building's daytime security guard, who just gave him a look and mouthed the words, "Easy money." Thomas nodded and smiled. "And you are…?" The kid stood up and extended his hand, which Thomas ignored.

"Eric. Eric—"

Thomas cut him off. "No last names, Eric. Here's your first tip of the night. When you're participating in illegal gambling operations the less anyone knows about you the better off we'll all be. Capiche?"

"Right, of course. Got any other tips for me?"

"Those you'll have to learn the hard way, my friend. And to the tune of a thousand dollars."

"But that's what it cost—oh—I see. Yeah, well, good luck, old man. I think I'll be keeping my money and everyone else's, here tonight."

Thomas laughed out loud and patted him on the shoulder. "You're a regular poker jerkoffs dot com super star, aren't you kid? I'll bet you an additional five hundred you don't make it to the final six." He raised his eyebrows and smiled at Mitch, whose eyes had widened as his friend contemplated the wager.

The new kid looked like he'd have to borrow the extra five bills from his mother, but to his credit, took his friend's unspoken advice, and declined the side bet. "Nah, that's okay. Taking a grand off you tonight is going to be sweet enough." He walked into the kitchen and cracked open a beer.

"Who's the frat boy, sucker? Friend of yours from your old college dropout days?"

"Funny, Tommy. He's just a guy I know from way back who won some cash playing online poker and thinks he's hot shit. I invited him to the game so he can see how to play real poker. Knock him down a peg, you know?"

"That's Mr. Van Steen, Mitch, and I thought they got rid of online poker?"

"They did, but only in The Land of the Free. Eric's a full on addict and he uses a proxy server that routes his accounts through Canada so he can play. Even has a Canadian bank account set up and everything."

"I don't know what's sadder, the fact that Americans can't play online poker for money or the fact that he can go to jail for doing what he's doing for about as long as I could for some of the shit I'm doing."

"We're a country that has is priorities all messed up, that's for damn sure. Fucking Republicans."

"Oh for the love of god, here we go with the left wing cries of inhumanity. You fucking bleeding heart pinko liberal commies are going to be the death of us, I swear." Thomas's face warmed and he clenched his fists, ready to dig in for a nice long argument, until Sidney slid into her seat at the table and diffused the situation before it took a nasty turn.

"Geez, you're just making friends all over the place tonight, aren't you?"

"Kiss my ass."

"Only if I can cop a feel of your man-boobs first."

"Old man gets burned," Eric quipped as he walked past on the way to his table.

Thomas jumped to his feet but Sidney stepped in front of him, handing him a deck of cards. "You're at that table with Frat Boy Slim. Draw for seats. Same rules as always. Each table plays until there are three left. Each player has the same number of chips as every other player at their table and each table has the same number of chips in play. When all the tables are down to three we'll consolidate to one table of six and play until there's only one person standing." Thomas nodded along with everyone around him. "As always, when it gets down to the final two they can decide to split the pot however they see fit should they not want to play it out. Early losers are welcome to stick around and have some drinks or watch the remaining players. Anyone caught giving signals or otherwise engaged in behavior unbecoming will the tied to a pole in the basement and whipped mercilessly across the face with my sex toys. Does everyone understand and agree to these terms?" Everyone either nodded or responded in the affirmative. "Great. There's fifteen thousand five hundred dollars at stake, gentleman. It's over there inside my humidor. Winner takes the cash, and because I'm such a good host, one of the Cuban cigars as well. That's not chump change and I don't need to remind you that what we're doing is most likely illegal. Good luck and happy pokering."

All the players took their seats and the games began. This was Thomas's eleventh visit to this particular event and many of the players were familiar. He was still raging from the cab driver, the construction magnate hitting on his wife and for her going along with it, and the new kid being a cocky sonofabitch. He did some breathing exercises his therapist taught him when he needed to calm down and get his blood pressure down. Angry poker was bad poker, and he was in the mood to win his sixth event, so bad wasn't going to cut it. He smiled at the thought of pocketing over ninety thousand tax free dollars in the last three years at the expense of all these liberal snowflakes. Punishing Frat Boy was his first goal, but after a few hands it was clear that the kid could actually play poker. Thomas made a mental note that he was at least as good as the top ten players that he knew well enough to make the comparison.

He and Mitch were the only two players who seemed to realize that they were playing a game within a game. They each needed to make sure they were in the final three at their table and that they had a good amount of chips if they were going to have a shot at winning. There was no use squeaking in to the final table at the number six spot if you showed up with not enough chips. The ante—a minimum bet every player must make before each hand— as well as the blinds—the amount by which the bets must raise—went up quickly. This was to prevent the games running too long. It also meant that if you wanted to stick around until the end that you needed to have a hefty stack of chips in front of you. If you didn't, you weren't out of the running, but you were definitely running uphill. There was no reward for playing a conservative game at Sidney's house. First place walked away with five digits in cash. Second place got a handshake.

Thomas paid the most attention to the new kid. It would have been foolish to pay the others no attention but they were familiar to him and with the exception of Mitch were an entirely different class of player. Most of them were regulars, but there were a couple, Frat Boy included, against whom he had never played. He knew what to look for and picked up on everyone's tells with relative ease. Eric was more difficult to suss out. It wasn't simply that he was new. He was so young. His only failing it would seem was the fact that he played almost exclusively online. As such, he was not as slick as he thought he was when playing with physical people. Thomas kept a close eye on him and made sure to make his move as one of the other new players placed a massive bet on a hand he was certain he was bluffing.

He not only called the bet but he also raised it by a significant amount. The new player hummed and hawed over it for a while but Thomas knew he would call. He was chasing a flush— five cards of all the same suit—but it didn't matter because Thomas was already sitting with a better hand. The odds of him losing were low. Very low.

The next player to act was Frat Boy, Eric. He called the big bet and Thomas beamed on the inside. Outside he was a rock. The guy who started the betting saw Thomas's raise. He didn't have much of a choice. He was committed and unless he wanted to lose all his credibility, he had to come along. The last card flipped over and Thomas could tell by the gleam in Eric's eye that he hit his card. The other active player didn't bet. Thomas paused for a few seconds and checked his cards one more time for dramatic effect. Then, he pushed all his chips into the center of the table.

"All in."

Both of Eric's eyebrows spiked upwards. "Okay. I think I have to call that bet." He moved his chips into the center of the table. "You've got me covered but we can do the math after I win."

The remaining player folded. "Too rich for my blood."

Thomas flipped over one of his cards—a jack that matched two other jacks showing on the table. Before he could flip over the other card, Eric flipped both his cards over to show a flush. He started to reach for the pot but Mitch, who was sitting to his left, stopped him. Thomas gave Mitch a nod of appreciation and flipped over his other card revealing a queen, which also paired nicely with another queen on the board, leaving a winning full house staring Frat Boy right in the face. Thomas took great enjoyment from the look on the kid's face and his slouched, utterly defeated posture. "Well, I guess we don't have to worry about doing the math now, do we, kid?"

Eric got up from the table, grabbed his jacket, and left without saying a word. Thomas looked over at Mitch and noticed a change in his facial expression. A slight tightening in his jaw maybe? Whatever it was, he took this as a good sign. From this moment on, he was in complete control. In spite of outward appearances, he knew he had the attention of everyone at the table, including his nemesis the security guard. The cards were going his way most of the time too, so that was helping a considerable amount. Poker was always easier when the cards cooperated. They could turn against you in a heartbeat, though, and often did, so you had to take advantage of it while you could.

Both Thomas and Mitch ended up at the final table with Thomas the chip leader. He scanned the other table and assessed the situation. He grabbed a beer and took a seat on the counter and watched the other table play it out. He knew all five players remaining. Three hands later he determined that it would be Sidney, Steve, and the guy everyone called Big Al. It was a not-so-clever nick name because of the fact that Big Al wasn't exactly suiting up for a football team anytime soon. Thomas took another long chug of beer and continued to watch in his estimation what was the slowest game of poker in the history of the world unfold hand after painstakingly boring hand. Tiredness began to set in. "Dear God, would something happen already." Sidney shot him a sideways glance. He blew her a kiss.

Two hands later he got his wish and there was some serious action at the table. Three players were betting hard and a small bead of sweat started to form on Big Al's forehead, a tell that was as obvious as it was disappointing.

He had seen comebacks before but this wasn't one. Then, in what could only be described as the boldest move of the night, after the second last card turned over, the diminutive man pushed all his chips in.

If Al's move was the boldest, then what happened next was the surprise of the evening. There were two callers, both with fewer chips than the man who pushed all in. "Save the math until after the cards fall, gentlemen. We don't have an Asian here to do it so we'll count it out on our fingers after." As with most of Thomas's racist comments, the room met this one with uncomfortable silence. Everyone flipped over their cards and it was pretty much a dead heat between all three players. The final card turned and one of the players hit his straight—five cards in consecutive number sequence—but the card also happened to be a diamond. Just the suit that Big Al needed to complete his ace-high flush.

Thomas jumped off the counter. "Holy shit, a double knockout! Ladies and gentlemen we have our final table."

The group took a break to clean up the table that they didn't need any more and collected some of the bottles and garbage that were littering Sidney's space. Thomas finished his beer. Once the table was clear and all the players were ready they drew for positions to start the final game. Thomas knew four of the other five players. Big Al, Steve-O, Mitch, and Sidney were regulars to the final table. Little Mike was a relative unknown to Thomas but he'd seen his face across from him at one game before. All were formidable opponents. He set his sights high, as he always did, but especially that night as he knew Brenda was going to be right properly pissed that he left the benefit. Even if she was flirting with the Italian construction guy, he knew her expectation was he would at least tell her before he left. As such, it was better to come home with a big pile of cash than it was empty handed.

The way it played out he may have well written the script for the evening. Aside from himself, Mitch and Sidney were the only ones remaining. It was Mitch's turn to deal. He rolled up his sleeves and revealed a fresh tattoo of a jewelled crown on his right forearm. "I thought you'd have wanted tattoos of pocket aces instead of the crown from the queen of hearts."

"Brave words from a guy who would probably pee his pants at the sight of a tattoo needle. It's for my girlfriend. My nickname for her is 'The Queen of Hearts' and her name is Jewell—like the singer, but with two 'Ls.'"

Sidney placed a large bet. "Awww, that's sweet." Mitch folded.

Thomas called. "Little Mitchy loves his bitchy so much he's turned into one."

Sidney took a long pull off the Cuban cigar she was smoking. "Do you have to work at being such an asshole, or does it just come naturally to you?"

"It just comes naturally to me, but I've made a point of working on it a little bit every day. I got my ten thousand hours of practice in before I hit twenty-five. I'm a full-fledged, black-belt ninja asshole now. Your bet."

"Check."

He looked down at his cards and decided to go for it. "All in." He pushed his stack of chips into the center of the table.

She took another puff, "Call," and flipped her cards over to reveal an ace and a ten, which matched the ones face up on the table, giving her two pair. He flipped his cards over to reveal the two black queens. There was still one common card to reveal and it was the queen of hearts. "Sorry, silly Sidney, but I guess it's just not your night." He dragged all the chips over to his side of the table. The game came down to a battle against his building security guard.

Mitch looked at the clock and then across to Thomas's massive stack of chips and then down to his feeble collection. "How about we call it done? You've got me covered at least six or seven times over so how about you let me take my entry fee back less fifty bucks so that everyone knows I at least contributed to the improvement fund?"

"How about no."

"Seriously? Fourteen thousand four hundred and fifty dollars in one night isn't enough for you? You just gotta have fifteen five. This is going to make a difference in your world?"

Thomas dealt the cards. "It's not about what makes the difference, it's about winning. It's about showing you I'm on top and always will be. You'll remember me kicking your ass and taking all your money much more than you'll remember a small token of kindness, and you'll be stronger for it after it's done. You might even be a better poker player for it, though I suspect you have probably peaked."

Mitch pushed all his chips into the center of the table. "All in."

"Oh, is that how it's going to be?"

"It is."

"Well, okay then." Thomas turned up five cards on the table and it was a mishmash of everything. There were no cards to build a straight with and all four suits showed, so there was no chance for a flush. There were no paired cards, either. "One at a time, for dramatic effect?"

"Okay, on three," Mitch agreed.

Thomas counted, "One, two... three," both players flipped over a card, and in both cases it was a two. Thomas cracked a nervous smile. "What are the odds we match on the second card too?"

A large puff of smoke and a big smoke ring floated across the table from Sidney. "About some huge number to one." There were two beats of silence. "What? I'm good at math."

He shook his head, returned his focus to the cards, and counted, "One, two... three." The players flipped over their cards and Mitch showed a king. Thomas had an ace. He surveyed the room and all the other opponents, especially the last one to lose, wore looks of "dissapanger"—a dangerous cross of disappointment and anger. He was pleased.

Mitch was not. "Congratulations, Captain Asshole. Take your money and get the hell out."

"This isn't even your house!"

The biggest smoke ring he'd ever seen drifted past his face. "Get out."

He walked over to the humidor, took the cash, and stuffed it into a brown paper bag. He put on his suit jacket, grabbed two cigars and slid them into the inside pocket next to his billfold, and did a little two-step before exiting through the front door.

*CHAPTER*SEVEN

Thomas awoke on the couch. "Hello?" he called out. He shuffled across the plush carpet toward the kitchen. The dishes on the sink indicated that Mother, who was sleeping, had eaten. Brittany spent the night at Sam's so he reasoned that it was Brenda who must have taken care of it before she left for wherever she was.

He sat back down on the couch and looked at the pile of cash on the coffee table, sighed, and went into his study to grab his briefcase. Sitting down in front of his money the familiar click of the dual locks opening echoed in the silent apartment. The total cash remaining was eight thousand and forty dollars. He put the two twenties into his billfold and wrapped an elastic band around the remaining eight thousand. With the penmanship of a grade school child he scratched a big "8" on a small sticky note and stuck it right over Ben Franklin's face.

Poker was lucrative but on occasion being an asshole cost him some money. In a painful twist, this was the first time it cost him cold hard cash that went straight to his wife. He shrugged it off, closed his briefcase, and made the decision to drop the money off at his safety deposit box. If he was lucky he might be able to sneak in some time with Nikki. He picked up the phone and called for a nurse to come over and keep an eye on his mother.

—

At the bank Thomas finally took the opportunity to count all of his poker winnings to date. Previously, he placed all his stacks of bills in his drawer with a colored sticky note on top. Yellow for rent payments from Mike that came in cash, blue for money that came in from other sources and would go out as allowance for Nikki, and pink for poker winnings, either from Mitch's game or at the casino.

In his private room with his safety deposit box open on the table he started to take out the bundles with the pink sticky notes on them and placed them in rows across the table. He mentally added all the numbers he had written down for each one. Not all of the stacks were the same value and he resisted the urge to organize it a bit better. He couldn't even remember putting together most of the bundles—and there were a lot of them.

Taxes were not something Thomas was fond of. Neither was jail, though. If pressed, he would admit that he hated taxes more than he hated jail, but he loved money more than he hated both of the other things. The numbers started to add up. Twenty thousand, thirty two thousand, fifty thousand…. With each bundle of cash that passed through his fingers his smile increased in proportion as well. Sixty-seven thousand, eighty-eight thousand, one-hundred-and-two thousand…. He assessed the piles that he had laid out on the table and tried to guess as to how much he had in total—all colours of sticky note combined. His guess was two million two hundred and twenty thousand. He looked up and all around and checked to see if he could see any cameras or microphones. He lived in a building with the most advanced surveillance he had ever seen in an apartment complex and it didn't do anything but make him more paranoid.

He continued to count. Within minutes he passed a million dollars. He did another check for cameras and even looked underneath the table on top of which sat all his money. He found nothing out of the ordinary. "Bitch," he said as he tossed the two bundles from his briefcase onto the pile with the other pink sticky notes. "One million eight hundred and twelve thousand. Huh, not a bad guess, Tommy boy." He ran his hands through his hair and stared at the piles. At some point he was going to need to get most of that into an offshore bank account but decided that for the time being it was as secure as it could be. His safety deposit box was getting a little snug. It was time to add another drawer.

He left the bank and headed to his car and thought about the allowance pile for Nikki. It was a pittance compared with the rest of the stacks. Still, it was his money and he might as well have a bit of fun with it. There was something that felt good about earning cold, hard cash and not paying a lick of taxes in the process. What felt even better was sharing the bed of a beautiful younger woman.

SATURDAY, JULY 8, 12:00 P.M.

Thomas picked up the phone and called Nikki. "Hey babe, I'm coming over in a few minutes. I have to tell you something."

"Sure, hun." She paused and for a brief moment he couldn't hear anything. *"I'm just tidying up the apartment so it's a bit of a mess."*

"Big party last night?" It was an accusation rather than a general inquiry.

Another pause. "Not exactly. I was looking for an earring that went missing and ended up tearing the place apart looking for it."

"One of the ones I gave you?"

Another pause. *"Of course, silly. Who else would be giving me fantastic jewelry?"*

Thomas decided to let it go. "I'll be there in thirty minutes."

Nikki's apartment was only a ten-minute drive if he got the lights. Fifteen if there was traffic. He got into his car and drove as fast as the stoplights and other drivers would allow, determined to get to Nikki's well in advance of his thirty-minute warning. As luck had it, he got all green lights and made great time. He arrived early enough to park around the corner and out of sight of any of her apartment windows. He used the secret spare key he had made up years ago and bounded up the stairs instead of waiting for the elevator. He placed his ear against the door and channeled all his listening power on the inside of the apartment. All he heard was Neil Diamond on the radio and Nikki singing along, horribly out of tune. The door to the apartment was locked but he opened it with his key and opened the door as quietly as it would allow. He tiptoed inside, shut the door behind him with a turn of the doorknob and a gentle press of his palm against the door, which better controlled the speed of it as it shut. He slipped off his shoes and walked toward the direction of the singing, making sure to peek into the other areas of the apartment looking for anything or anyone out of place or suspicious.

The door to the bathroom was only open a few inches, but it was enough to give him a view of her elbow, her leg, and her cute little feet standing in front of the vanity. He peered into her bedroom, stepped in, and had a look under her bed and in her closet. He found nothing of interest and stepped back into the hallway, pushing the door to the bathroom wide open. Nikki was standing over the sink brushing her teeth in the nude, froth from her toothpaste spilling from the corner of her mouth and dripping down her chin as she tried to belt out the lyrics to "Cracklin' Rosie."

"Wha da—holy phuck! You scared da libing shit outa me!" She pointed the toothbrush at his face and speckles of minty-scented white paste speckled the front of his shirt. She spat into the sink and rinsed her mouth by scooping some water up from the faucet with her hand. She closed the door in his face and when she opened the door again he was still standing in place. She pursed her lips and ignored his pouting. She turned sideways, stepped past him, and walked into the bedroom as he took a good long look at her naked form gliding across the floor.

"You said you were going to be half an hour. I thought I had time to shower and pretty myself up."

"You got your shower in, and you can pretty yourself up later. Besides, from what I can see you're pretty just the way you are."

Nikki's cheeks turned a familiar shade of pink. "You're just saying that because I'm naked."

Thomas looked her up and down and saw the perfectly smooth curves of a woman half his age. His legs turned to jelly and his penis did just the opposite. He pushed her down onto the bed, got down on his knees, and pushed hers apart.

She covered herself with her hands. "I thought you had something you wanted to talk to me about. A brilliant idea or something."

"I just got a better idea. At least for the moment. Now move your hands. You've been a bad girl and I should give you a talking to."

"A talking to?"

"Yeah, you're in for a real tongue-lashing." He needed less than five minutes to get her over the finish line. Once convinced that she was satisfied he lay beside her on the bed, ran a finger from her neck down to her belly button, and then back up again.

She turned her head and purred into his ear. "I have a hard time believing you're going to have a better idea than that one today."

"Well how does a couple million dollars in cash and a little cabin on a Caribbean island sound?"

Nikki sat up. "Come again?"

"I haven't even come once, and after that performance you'd think I'd at least get some reward."

"You've got my undying gratitude and affection, and almost unfettered access to this." She pointed between her legs.

"Let me tell you a story about a guy with a lot of money and a girl he wants to share it with." She sat cross-legged facing him and urged him to sit up. He acquiesced and she took his hands in hers. "Once upon a time a guy started cooking his books so he could squirrel away cash from his real estate empire and give his girlfriend a healthy allowance, in addition to all other fine things he bestowed upon her on a regular basis. Only he was accumulating money faster than either of them could spend it. In addition to that, he had some other tax-free cash income coming in, as well as some modest poker winnings."

"That sounds like a lot of money."

"It is, and here's the best part. In addition to that, our prince has an offshore account under a dummy corporation. Between that money and the cash, and the fact that he makes the absolute best real estate deals, he figures he and his girlfriend can retire somewhere warm and sunny together."

"Oooo, I like this story. Tell me, kind sir, where does one keep—I'm sorry how much cash does this fabulous man have? Did you say two million dollars?"

"Right now it's a hair over one point eight."

"Holy Hannah, that's a lot of cash. Where does one keep that kind of money? Storage locker down at the gym?"

"Ha ha! Not exactly. I have a safety deposit box down at the bank." He pulled his car keys out of his pocket and pointed to an odd-shaped one. "Along with several other safeguards, if you don't have this, you don't get the money."

"What's stopping you from leaving right now and taking me with you?"

"I still have my mother to care for. I couldn't possibly leave her with my soon to be ex-wife. I'd never be able to live with myself knowing that I didn't do everything possible for her while she was still with us."

"She's the only person in the world you've ever loved, isn't she?"

He looked her in the eye and then kissed her forehead. "Until you."

"That's the sweetest thing anyone's ever said to me. Can I see it?"

"Sure." His eyes struggled to fixate anywhere but her chest or between her legs. He took the key off his keychain and ran the end of it slowly around her nipple, and then the other one, before tracing a path down past her belly button and to the top of her pubic bone. She reached down and put her hand on top his.

"Not the key, silly. The money. Can you go take me to see the money?"

"You want to go see the money?"

"Yes."

"You can count it for me."

"I was thinking we could do more than just count."

"That's the spirit. Now throw on some clothes. Something nice, not yoga pants or something like that."

Nikki folded her arms in protest. "But you're wearing just a t-shirt and jeans."

"Trust me, babe. For this you're going to want to look a certain part. Wear a skirt. No panties, and put on some blouse or something. And put on that necklace I gave you a while back."

"No panties, how is that possibly going to make a difference to the bank?"

"It won't. I just like the idea of you going commando."

—

The pair walked straight to the attendant at the bank and Thomas showed his key to the gentleman behind the counter. "I'd like to visit my safety deposit box, please."

"Very good, Mr. Van Steen. If you could just enter your code into the pin pad for me please."

Thomas punched in his code and Nikki pretended not to notice as he punched in *6699*. A green light flashed on top of the unit.

"Very good, sir. If you'd please come with me. Ma'am, you can have a seat here and one of my colleagues would be happy to bring you something to drink."

Thomas turned to the attendant. "Oh, she'll be coming with me."

The concierge cocked his head a bit to one side and gave a slight nod to him. "Very well, Mr. Van Steen. If you'll both please follow me."

They walked down a long hallway and down a flight of spiral stairs with an ornate carved handrail. At the bottom of the stairs was a small landing area with a table and chair, presumably for a guard. A large steel door loomed beside the chair. The attendant punched in a code on a keypad on the wall and turned a large dial to open the door. Inside another large room with three walls of boxes of various sizes, showcased brass plates with numbers engraved on them. He handed Thomas a key with the number four on it.

"Here you go, sir. When you've retrieved your box you can take it to viewing room number four through that door and on your right. I'll be closing the door but I won't lock it. I'll be outside the door sitting in the chair. Just come out when you're done."

"Thank you."

The attendant left and closed the door behind him. Thomas walked over to box 246, slid in the key, and gave it a turn. He swung the door open and exposed a locker with a shelf and a large metal box underneath it. He grabbed the handle and picked it up, closed the door, and locked it with the key.

"Why'd you lock the empty locker thingy?" She pointed to the box.

"It's a good habit to get into in the event I have more than just a box full of cash stored in there. Secondly, if someone else comes in while we're in the viewing room I'd rather they not know what box is mine. Just in case."

"Paranoid much?"

He gave her a sideways glance and they walked out of the deposit box room and into Viewing Room Number Four. It was a small room with a black velvet topped table with two leather chairs in it. The carpeting was a tight weave but soft under foot. The lights were quite bright but attached to a dimming switch. Thomas turned the lights down a bit. The walls were bare and undecorated but painted a pleasant color. Sort of the beige version of green. He closed the door behind him, placed the box on the table, and opened the lid and Nikki got her first look at the cash.

"Holy shit, that's a lot of money." She reached in and grabbed two bundles from the top of the pile and held them up closer to her face.

"And there's more being added all the time. I figure by the time we're ready to take off I can add a few hundred thousand more, plus whatever I can weasel into the offshore account." He took a step closer to her and wrapped his arms around her waist. "How'd you like to have money rain down on you while you put a big smile on my face?"

She turned around and dropped to her knees and he undid the elastic on a bundle of cash. He started to drop hundred dollar bills down onto her head as it bobbed back and forth below his waist. She started to pick them up off the floor and rub them all over her body. Thomas only got halfway through the other bundle before he finished and she stood up and gave him a smile, wads of hundred dollar bills still clutched her hand. Some were sticking out of her bra. She reached between her legs and pulled another hundred out from her skirt. His eyebrows bolted upwards. "Jesus Christ. Just when I thought the smell of money couldn't get any better."

"You're such a pervert."

"Yeah, but I'm a rich pervert. Now what say you help me clean up this mess?"

She started to add the bills to the stack and he took it from her. He reached down and rubbed it between her legs, causing her to get up on her tiptoes to stabilize herself while using the table for support. She was always ready for a quick second orgasm if she could be aroused shortly after her first.

From the look on her face, it would appear that he had not missed his window of opportunity. "I can't decide what you're more of, rich or perverted."

Thomas used his whole hand to massage her between her legs with Franklin's face the only obstacle preventing his fingers from penetrating. She came quickly and quietly, which was a good thing as the bill started to show considerable signs of wear from all the rubbing and the moisture.

Shaking and biting her lower lip Nikki stood in front of the table trying to gain her composure. "Well, that answers that question."

He smiled, folded the bill in half, and placed it in the middle of his solid gold monogrammed billfold.

She looked at him with a coy seductiveness that he had not seen from her in quite some time. "Don't go using that to tip the doorman or anything, you hear me?"

"Don't worry, babe. I plan to keep it in a safe place and always nearby. I'll take it out whenever I want to be reminded of the two things I love the most."

"Aw, that's sweet of you to say. But which one do you love more?"

He stood in front of her transferring his weight from one foot to the other. "Tied for first."

"Mhmm."

They tidied up the cash and put it all in its rightful spot in the box—minus one hundred dollars—and returned the box to its locker. Thomas handed him the key to the viewing room. "Thank you very much. Now, if it's not too much trouble I have a favor to ask."

"Of course, sir. How can I be of service?"

He put his arm around Nikki. "I'd like to have Nikki added to the access list for my safety deposit box. No extra key required, but I'd like for her to be able to retrieve things in the event I need to travel and I leave the key with her."

The attendant swallowed hard and managed a forced, but polite enough reply. "No problem at all, sir. We'll just go upstairs and fill out a bit of paperwork."

Nikki interlocked her arms around one of Thomas's and squealed with delight. "Oh. Em. Gee! You are just the sweetest man in the world."

The three went upstairs and Nikki and the attendant sat at a large desk while Thomas stood and turned himself to face the tellers.

"Now, Miss…."

"Carcillo."

"Now, Miss Carcillo. All we'll need from you is some basic information and a piece of ID and we'll get you into the system and you can select your access number."

Thomas put his hand on her shoulder. "Listen, babe. I'm just going to go over to the teller for a bit. Just meet me at the front door when you're done."

"Sure thing honey."

"We'll just be a couple minutes, Mister Van Steen, and then a signature from you before you go."

Thomas walked up to an open teller.

"Good afternoon, sir, how can I help you today?"

He handed over his bankcard and a piece of ID to the young woman behind the glass. "I'd like to make a withdrawal please, checking account."

"Very good Mr. Van Steen, for what amount?"

"Twenty-five thousand dollars please. Large bills. Preferably in bundles of five thousand."

"I see." She fidgeted with her pen. "I'm going to have to go get the manager."

"That's fine, I'm in no hurry."

The teller walked away with his bankcard and ID and around the corner. She returned with the manager. "Mr. Van Steen, Allison informs me you'd like to withdrawal a large sum of money, and have it bundled."

Thomas folded his arms across his chest. "That's correct."

"Well, you see it's a bit of an unusual request, I was just wondering if we could electronically transfer it for you instead. It is much safer, rather than have you walking around with a bag of cash."

Thomas put his hands on the counter and leaned on the heels of his hands, spreading his fingers wide on the cool marble surface. "Your opinion, while interesting, is unfortunately not worth the air it took you to share it. Please provide me with my money before I take the tens of millions of dollars my company sends through your bank every year and electronically transfer them to the bank down the street."

The manager pursed his lips. "Of course, sir. Be right with you."

The manager returned with a small black velvet bag and five bundles of hundred dollar bills. He placed the bundles on the counter and picked one back up holding it at an angle so Thomas could get a better look. "Sir, as you can see, each bill is a hundred dollar denomination. Each bundle has a wrap with the bundle total, in this case, five thousand dollars, printed on it. Five bundles at five thousand dollars. Just so you know, the bills are sequential and we have recorded the numbers."

Thomas looked the manager in the eyes. "Not that it matters, but why did you do that?"

The manager didn't break eye contact. "In the event you needed us to, sir. Will there be anything else I can do for you?"

"As a matter of fact, there is. Can you get me an account printout for the last two weeks for the checking account that I hold joint with my daughter? Same for my wife."

"Certainly, Miss Aalto here will be able to help you with that."

She typed a few keystrokes on the computer and walked over to the printer, returning with four pages of papers. She handed them to him.

He looked through the pages for any transactions that stood out. Brittany spent too much money on alcohol and Starbucks but it was otherwise in order. Brenda on the other hand, seemed to be writing checks at a furious pace. He made a mental note to pull the checks and see what nonsense she was spending his money on.

He felt a pair of arms around his waist and spun around to Nikki beaming ear-to-ear. "Thomas, have I told you how much I love you?"

"No, but you showed me about fifteen minutes ago." He patted his pocket that contained his billfold. In the car he reached into his velvet bag and handed her two bundles of cash. "Don't go spending that all in one place, you hear me?" With wide eyes and a smile to match she leaned over and gave him a big hug and a kiss on the cheek.

*CHAPTER*EIGHT

Thomas returned home from his visit to the bank and his encounter with Nikki, having given her an additional allowance for being such a good sport. Ten thousand dollars should buy him a little leeway in terms of time with her. Many details still needed sorting before he could run away to a desert island though. The business had to be sold, he had to make plans to get himself, Nikki, and all the cash out of the country, he had to ensure that his gold-digging wife and his entitled daughter got as little as possible in the process, and it all had to wait until Mother was no longer of this Earth.

Coming up from the parking garage to the main floor to get the mail, he noticed Mitch at the security station. "Hey there Mitchy boy. I've got fifteen thousand five hundred and two reasons why I'm in a good mood today. How about you? You appear to be working for the weekend so you must be thrilled."

"Good morning, Mr. Van Steen. There are always many reasons for me to be happy. Thank you for asking."

Not deterred by Mitch's kill-him-with kindness approach he continued the assault. "I mean, I can lose a grand in five minutes at the casino and not bat an eyelash. It's a good thing they make you wear that uniform so you don't have to worry about work clothes." He tugged on the lapels of his two thousand-dollar suit.

Mitch smiled but not in a way that gave Thomas confidence it was sincere. "What do you mean by fifteen thousand five hundred and two? The two cigars you took instead of just the one?"

"Ha! I completely forgot about those. No, Mitch, my friend, one of those reasons involves a fine woman and the other one involves seeing you wasting your Saturday night working after I took your money so easily last night." He shot him a smirk and a wink, and left him to sit dejected at the desk. Arriving upstairs with his velvet bag of fifteen thousand dollars cash, he went into the kitchen to get a drink and then into his office to grab his briefcase. He wandered the apartment for a bit to draw the attention of his wife, who was puttering around preparing the table for supper.

Once convinced he had her interested, he sat down on the couch, opened his briefcase, and carefully placed the three bricks of cash inside. He made sure to close the briefcase with more force than necessary and locked it, placing it on the floor in front of the end table.

Brittany was especially talkative at dinner. "How was your evening?"

"No complaints. The event went off without a hitch, but your father ditched me to go play poker. I was mad until I saw how much money he won. It paid for the art I bought at the silent auction and a couple pairs of some delightful Jimmy Choos."

The mention of art and shoes sat her up in her seat. "Choos that might fit a certain daughter?"

"Choos that cost so much a certain daughter will be lucky if she even gets to hold them, let alone wear them out of the apartment."

Thomas kept his head down and ate his dinner. Shoe talk was not something for which he was equipped to participate, nor art, for that matter. "What about your old pair? The brown and gold ones."

"Possibly. What's the occasion?"

"Sam and I are going to a gallery tonight. A friend of a friend has a show or something. I want to look fabulous."

Thomas looked up from his plate. "We're all about art in this family, aren't we? Let her wear the shoes. At least with those we can be sure she won't sell them for cash."

He gave Brittany a sideways glance and Brenda shot him an icicle stare and, while still looking at him, said to Brittany, "I suppose it couldn't hurt. They're in my closet. You can grab them after supper."

"Awesome! Tonight is going to be epic, thank you. Now, tell me about this art you purchased. It would be totes hilarious if it was done by the guy who was opening tonight."

"If he's local, then for sure not. It's from some Scandinavian I've never heard of. To be honest I'm not sure it's all that great a piece. It might just be so bad that it's good. I was a few cocktails in when I bid and I was ticked I was stranded—" she turned her head to Thomas "—so the details are a bit foggy. I think I remember something about a robot on a swing."

"Oh my god, you bought an Algot Björkman?"

"Yeah, that's it! That's not your friend, is it?"

Thomas rolled his eyes. "Algor Brooktrout?"

"Not my friend, but I can't believe you don't know who he is. His stuff is all the rage right now. If he dies anytime soon his stuff will be worth a fortune."

Thomas looked up from his plate, put his fork down on the edge, and wiped the corners of his mouth with his napkin. "Well, we bought one, well your mother did at least—I just paid for it—and this fellow is still alive so we're stuck with it."

"Get over it, Thomas. It was for a good cause. I don't have to remind you that had you been present you would have had ample opportunity to talk me out of it."

"Seriously?" Brittany was excited. "Like, what'd you pay for it? I heard one of his pieces went for almost fifty grand at an auction last month."

Brenda jumped in before Thomas could swallow his mouthful of lasagna. "Well we didn't pay anywhere near that for our piece. I think it was fifteen thousand. One-five."

"Wow! That's, like, practically a steal for one of his paintings, especially if it has a robot in it. Those are his most sought after."

Thomas pointed his fork in her direction. "Robots? Robots are his most sought after paintings?" Bits of lasagna flew across the table.

Brittany nodded. "Uh huh. Robots. Ever since they landed that rover on Mars robots have been all the rage. The Japanese are making a fucking fortune off of it."

Thomas shoveled another forkful of lasagna into his mouth. "Yeah, and at least one fucking Scandinavian."

Brenda slammed her hand down on the table. "Language! Both of you! We were having a perfectly civil conversation about art until you both piped up with your potty mouths."

Thomas and Brittany shared a rare but brief moment of solidarity as they hung their heads and tried not to giggle. Brittany took a big gulp of milk as he continued. "This lasagna can't be sullied by profanity. It's fucking amazing."

Brittany spit choke laughed, spraying milk all over her place at the table. Small drips fell out of her nose. An avalanche of laughter came from Thomas.

Brenda stood up and slammed both hands down on the table, knocking over Brenda's glass and spilling what was left of her milk. "That's enough! Both of you! This is not a frat party and this is not poker night with the boys. Now finish your meals. And get something to clean up this mess."

Brittany got up from the table, picking up her glass and plate of lasagna with a side of milk. "I'm done anyway. I have to get ready for the gallery opening. Mom, can I still borrow your shoes?"

Brenda sat down and held up her hands in mock prayer, then palms to the ceiling in exasperation and defeat. "Fine." She lowered her head into her hands and stared down at her half-eaten dinner.

Thomas took this opportunity to stand and pick up his plate as well. "I am going in to see if Mother is in any condition to eat and have a conversation." Just then, the power went off and alarm bells started to ring from his mother's room.

"Shit, who didn't plug mother back into the backup power socket?"

"Not me. I make a point not to touch anything when I go in there. I'm afraid I'll screw up one of the machines."

"Brenda?"

"Oh, as if, Thomas. Seriously? It was probably the cleaning company. They're sending over a new person every damn week anyway." The alarm bells continued to ring throughout the apartment. "Well, shouldn't you be getting in there and doing something about it?"

"Oh, shut your piehole. Batteries will keep her going for about half an hour. It won't take me that long to get in there, even with your goddamn nattering. And for Christ's sake, call the cleaning company first thing Monday morning and give them right proper hell."

She gave him a fake salute and stood, picking up her vodka tonic with her other hand. "Aye-aye, captain!"

Thomas walked into his mother's room and she was awake in bed and trying to reach over toward one of her machines. Thomas intervened. "Mother, just lie down. I'll take care of this." He got down on his knees and checked the plug on the main unit. As suspected, he found it plugged into the wrong socket. He unplugged it from the plain white socket and plugged it into the adjacent one with the orange-ringed edging around each of the outlets.

Thomas pulled up a chair and sat beside his mother's bed and rubbed her forehead just like she used to do when he was a small child and home nursing an illness. Her face relaxed and he could see a small smile forming underneath her breathing mask.

He lifted it off her mouth a little and she whispered to him. "Thank you." A tear formed in the corner of his eye and rolled down his cheek. He took her hand and patted the top of it.

"Would you like to try some real food, mother?" She gave an affirming nod.

"Okay then, I'll be right back. Cereal okay?" Another nod.

Thomas headed into the kitchen and realized that the water cooler with the hot water tap was not working due to the power outage. The stove was gas-powered though, and with that, he pulled his Zippo out of his pocket, turned on one of the burners, and lit it. Placing a small pot of water on the burner, he stood patiently and waited for it to boil. Once the water boiled, he turned off the burner and poured some of the water into a bowl filled with Pablum. He would have liked to feed her oatmeal but sometimes the oats stuck in her the mouth and throat, and the thought of his mother struggling terrified him.

Returning to the bedroom, his mother was attentive at the prospect of something other than an intravenous supper. Thomas propped her up on a set of spare pillows and set the bowl in her lap. He lifted her mask and spooned some of the mushy cereal into her mouth. The frail woman looked content for the first time in weeks. He returned the mask to her face and stirred the bowl.

"It's not too hot, is it?" She shook her head. "Good. Now here comes another spoonful." He used a tone that one normally took while feeding a baby. His mother raised an eyebrow and pursed her lips. "Okay, okay. I get your point. Not funny." Thomas lifted the mask again. "You never did understand my sense of humor, did you?"

"No."

She kept her mouth open to accept another serving. Thomas looked into the bowl. "This stuff isn't exactly your favourite, is it?" His mother shrugged her shoulders and looked over at the IV drip. Thomas nodded. "Ah yes, better than the alternative, I suppose." His mother accepted another spoonful of food. This continued until the bowl was half-empty and she shook her head "no" when he asked her if she wanted any more. "Okay, we're done. That was good for a change. You must be tired." A nod in the affirmative that time. "Would you like me to read to you for a while?" Nod. "This book here? Dickens?" Nod. Thomas picked up the ancient hardcover and started to read. "It was the best of times, it was the worst of times—"

He read to her for half an hour, long after she had fallen asleep. He put a bookmark where he stopped and placed the book on the night table before tiptoeing out of the room and closing the door, leaving it open just a crack.

In the bedroom, Brenda was getting dressed in jeans and a fancy t-shirt. In a casual tone he said, "Heading out, are ya?"

"Going out with the girls to a comedy club. Upright Citizen's Brigade. It's supposed to be funny. You wouldn't know."

"Har-dee-har-har." He stuffed his hands in his pants pockets. "I was thinking of going out with Mike for a few drinks and maybe catch the end of the hockey game. Ottawa is in town and the Rangers love beating up on those guys."

"Whatever, dear. The nursing company's number is on the fridge. They usually need an hour's notice. More if you want someone specific."

Thomas checked his watch. "Aw crap, no way I'm going to make it. Maybe I'll have Mike over here instead."

Brenda folded her arms across her chest. "I don't like it when he comes over here. He always smells like marijuana and he's got a foul mouth."

"He's my friend, Brenda. He got me out of more than a couple binds when I was growing up, and especially in college. It's the least I can do. Without the job I gave him and the occasional visit here to watch the big screen, who knows what he'd be doing. Probably selling drugs instead of smoking them."

Brenda chuckled. "It's good to see you aren't blinded by your friendship."

"What's that supposed to mean?"

"Nothing, dear." She patted him on the shoulder as she grabbed her purse and headed out for the night. "Enjoy your evening with "smoking 'em, not selling 'em" Mike. Tell him he has to go outside if he wants to smoke anything while he's here, and I mean anything, and preferably not any of that vile green stuff. That goes for you as well."

Thomas took his turn at a fake salute and grabbed his cell phone out of his pocket and called Mike. "Mikey! How do you feel about grabbing a couple six packs on your way over here to watch the game? The Sens are in town and I know how much you hate those bastards."

"I dunno, man, I'm kinda busy."

"Oh, I'm sure you can find a free hour in your busy schedule. Maybe I should speak to your assistant instead?"

"An assistant! Now that's the best idea I've heard all day."

"Keep it in your pants, Casanova. It ain't gonna happen. Speaking of pants put some on and get your sorry ass over here. The game's already started."

"All right, be right over. Be forewarned, I'm wearing my New York Rangers boxer shorts with "He shoots! He scores!" *written across the crotch and they will be making an appearance every time we get a goal."*

—

Mike entered the building and Mitch was still working. Mike approached him, hands full of beer, and bags of nacho chips, cheese sauce of questionable providence, and salsa hot enough to melt your fillings. "What's up, Security Dude Mitch. Sucks to be you working tonight, huh?"

Mitch looked up from his Rolling Stone magazine. "Oh hello there, Cheech. Or is it Chong? I can never remember."

"I'd give you the finger but as you can see I've got my hands full. Or you would be able to see if you were paying attention. Some freaking security guard you are."

Mitch looked back down at his magazine and gave Mike the finger. "My hands aren't holding a week's worth of food for the munchies, so I can give you the finger. I did it in slow motion so you wouldn't miss it. Weed dulls the reflexes and I wanted to make sure you got the full effect."

"I'm here to see Thomas. Mr. Van Steen to you, of course."

Mitch let out an exasperated sigh and put his magazine down on his keyboard. He grabbed a leather log book from under the desk and placed it on the top of the counter. "I'm going to need to get you to sign the visitor's log, Willie Nelson."

Mike held up both his hands, showing Mitch that they were in fact still full of beer and bags of food.

Mitch shrugged and put the pen in the crease of the log book. "I'll just need your full name, date, and time of visit, expected duration of your stay, apartment number you'll be visiting, and a signature. Mmmmkay? Thanks."

Mike glared at Mitch. His right eye twitched as he put down the twelve pack of beer that he was holding in his left hand. "You're a real pain in the ass, you know that?" Mike scribbled down the required information into the log book and pocketed the pen.

"So I've been told."

Mitch pulled another pen out of the drawer and placed it in the crease of the book before sliding it back under the desk. "I'll call up to Mr. Van Steen, your BFF Thomas, and let him know you're on your way up."

Upstairs, Mike entered the apartment without knocking. Thomas was sitting in his giant chair and already drinking a beer. "Hey, I thought you told me to bring beer?" Mike protested as he put two six packs in the fridge and the rest of the bags on the counter.

"I never said I didn't have beer, just that you should bring some. We don't take kindly to freeloaders 'round these parts."

Mike started to pre-heat the oven. "That's harsh, man. If I wasn't such a nice guy I'd consider not giving you any of my specialty nachos."

"My colon would thank you."

Mike stepped out of the kitchen long enough to throw a lime at Thomas. He missed and it careened off a lampshade, knocking the remote control off the armrest.

"Asshat. Plus, your aim is shit."

Mike made a jerk off motion with his hand. "Special nacho cheese for you."

"What was that?"

"Nachos, coming up in ten minutes!"

Sitting in front of the game, Thomas and Mike ate nachos and drank beer. The sight was about as primitive as possible for the twenty-first century. After devouring an entire pan of nachos and three beers Thomas decided it was time to head to the washroom. "Hey man, I gotta go use the men's room. If you need to go you can go to the bathroom down the hall on the right."

"Okie dokie." Mike raised his beer and toasted the air. The visiting Senators were shellacking the Rangers. Halfway through the third period, with the nachos long gone and seven empty beer bottles in front of him, Mike decided to head home for the evening. "Well, man, I think I'm calling it a night. The shitty Rangers aren't coming back from this debacle of a game and I went pretty hard last night so I'm calling it."

"Pussy."

"Yeah, well you are what you eat, I guess."

"Asshole."

"Now, that's just wishful thinking on your part."

Thomas reached down beside him, picked up the lime Mike threw earlier, and chucked it at his head. It hit him right between the eyes. On instinct, he rubbed the spot with his hand. "Fuck! Ow! Dick. That's going to leave a mark."

"It already did. I'll be sure to let the judges of your next beauty contest know it was my fault."

Mike slammed the door on his way out.

*CHAPTER*NINE

Thomas sat in his big recliner and watched sports highlights from the night before split screen with the soccer game happening over in Manchester. Brenda walked in from a workout in their home gym, stood beside his chair, and surveyed the mess. He looked up from his coffee at her standing beside him in her active wear. "Why the hell didn't you come to bed last night?"

"I didn't appreciate coming home from an otherwise wonderful evening to a complete disaster of a house, so I went to the guest room, which is in pristine condition since we never have guests over."

"I was going to clean up but got tired and went to bed."

"I almost broke my neck on a lime coming into the house, Thomas. A lime. There was a lime on the floor of my hallway."

"A lime?"

"Don't be smart. I'm going to take a shower."

"Did you want some company?" He looked her up and down and winked.

"I'm good, thanks. Clean up your crap."

Thomas half-heartedly tidied up the living room, piling most of his garbage onto two plates and the empty platter, which he balanced on top of his arm with one plate in each hand. Dumping the pile onto the kitchen counter, he began the process of sorting the garbage from the compost from the recyclables before thinking better of it and tossing the whole lot into a black garbage bag. He opened the fridge to get a glass of juice and saw the lime sitting by itself in the middle of a shelf. "Very nice. Passive aggressive Brenda, one, Thomas, zero." He grabbed the lime and tossed it into the garbage bag. "Tie game."

He brewed another cup of coffee and went to his office. Closing the door, he fired up his laptop and started looking at jewelry for Nikki. A stunning green, heart-shaped emerald necklace surrounded by two rows of brilliant blue sapphires reminded him of an island. He bought it and hoped that it would keep Nikki's eyes on the prize as she waited for the planets to align. He turned his attention to researching private islands in the Caribbean. A simple search for "private Caribbean islands for sale" turned up quite a few useful results. Depending on where the island was, real estate rules and taxes were all different. He had people who could sort all that stuff out so instead focused on what he wanted in a permanent getaway.

Airstrip or fly-in was mandatory, as was at least one beach. It also had to be developed—there was no way he was going to eat the cost of having to ship in supplies and workers. At first glance he found quite a number of properties in either the South Pacific or Caribbean that looked promising. He picked up his desk phone and called his accountant. "Christian, it's Thomas."

"Hello, Mr. Van Steen, what can I do for you?"

"Christian, I need to move some stuff around and make a large purchase."

"Of course. What level of obfuscation is required? Are you making a bold statement or do you want this to fly a little more under the radar?"

"The latter. I need this to be practically untraceable."

"As you know, sir, the bigger the transaction the harder it is to—well, shall I say, to maintain discretion."

"Compared to some of the stuff going on with Russia, this is small potatoes. Small potato-ish. Look, we have an agreement, a pretty good one, I think. You keep my books and oversee financial transactions. In exchange for your expertise and discretion I pay you large sums of money."

"I understand, sir. Of course. I didn't mean to imply that it was an impossible task. I just wanted you to be aware of the risks. What's the transaction you would like me to oversee?"

"I want you to buy me an island."

"I'm sorry, did you just say you want to purchase an island?"

"Yes. An island."

"Any island? As a vacation home?"

"In a manner of speaking. More of a permanent vacation home, if you get my drift."

"I see, and is there any intent on making any income with this property?"

"Nope."

"Hmm."

"Can we do it? I know we can do it but I want you to tell me we can do it."

"How much are we talking? I have to admit, I don't have the foggiest idea what a private island in the Caribbean costs, or what the real estate laws are down there. Tax laws I know inside and out, and we'll be leveraging them to make this happen, but real estate outside of North America and a few parts of Europe is a black hole to me."

"It depends on a lot of factors and there's quite a range."

"Ballpark it for me."

"Really, when you think about it, I'd be getting an entire island. That's got to be worth it, right?"

"How much?"

"Somewhere around forty million."

"We can do that. Have you talked with your lawyer yet?"

"Not yet. I wanted to talk to the numbers guy before I talked to the legal guy. No use going to the legal guy if there's a problem with the numbers, you know?"

"Of course, I'll enlist the help of your real estate agent, the one who you worked with for your last casino development project and start to put a short list together. I'll make sure all the finances are in order, and of course keep all of this on the QT. It's probably going to take a while."

"We've got time, not to worry. Mother is still with us and even doing a bit better these days."

"Well, that's great to hear. Is there anything else you want to discuss?"

"No, that's all for now, Christian. Thanks for your loyalty. Sorry to bother you on a Sunday morning like this." He hung up and returned his attention to his private island search results and tried to imagine Nikki sunbathing in the nude as he walked toward her on their private beach with a bottle of champagne and two glasses on one hand and a bottle of suntan lotion in the other. He closed his eyes and heard nothing but the sound of the waves crashing and felt nothing but the cool breeze on his skin and the warm sun on the top of his head.

He gasped for breath and felt his heart skip a beat when a loud pounding on the door interrupted his island fantasy. "Thomas! Did you seriously just throw out dishes instead of putting them in the dishwasher?"

"Yes."

"Well, get your butt out here and clean this up properly. Seriously. The maids are here every week and you still manage to leave this place a disaster for them."

He slouched over his keyboard and took another look at the azure waters of the Caribbean Sea surrounding a brilliant green island and thought of the necklace he just purchased for Nikki. He sighed. "Yes, dear."

SUNDAY, JULY 9, 6:00 P.M.

Come dinnertime, Thomas was still sulking about his argument with Brenda. She wasn't a fan of being "yes dear'd" and it wasn't in his nature to apologize—even if he was wrong. He spent most of the day holed up in his office looking at tropical island properties and the two hadn't so much as said a peep to each other in almost eight hours. Making his way out of the office, smells of dinner hit him. Even if she was pissed off, he could still count on his wife to make dinner. He turned the corner into the kitchen and there were two plates of food sitting on the counter. The meat and vegetables had steam rising from them. The division of labor was simple—she did the cooking, and he was supposed to set the table and clean up afterwards. He went into the cutlery drawer and pulled out two knives and two forks and set a pair of them down beside one of the plates. "Table's set." He picked up the other plate and turned to exit the kitchen.

"Seriously?" She put her hands on her hips and raised both eyebrows.

He shuffled his plate over to the hand holding the cutlery and reached around her to open the cupboard door adjacent to her head. He pulled out a wine glass from the shelf, closed the door, brought his arm back around to her other side, and placed it on the counter beside her cutlery. "There. Now the table's set." He turned and exited the kitchen and strolled back to his office. He didn't even care that he forgot to grab himself a beer. He briefly pondered going back for one but felt that his exit was a mic drop moment and returning to the scene would ruin the effect. Sitting down at his desk, he typed in his password and resumed searching for island properties.

—

With his stomach sated and his cutlery folded neatly on one side of the white china dish, he got up, locked the door, and returned to his desk. Opening up a private browser that wouldn't keep his search history, he navigated to his favorite porn site and started scrolling through the various videos. A blonde-haired woman wearing nothing but high heels and a smile caught his attention and it reminded him of Nikki so he picked up his phone and snapped a picture of the bulge in his pants and sent it to her in a text message. He didn't have to wait long for her reply.

N: Nice. Who is this?

In turn, it didn't take him long to get angry, forget about what was on his browser, and respond back.

T: What the hell do you mean who is this? It's Thomas! Who the hell else could it be?

N: I know, silly. I was just teasin'

T: Well, you have to put a smiley face or a winky face on the end of your message so I know you're being cheeky.

N: Oh, okay. I was going to ask you what you were up to but I can already see that you've found a way to occupy yourself for a while. Where is *she*?

T: Ugh. She's being a pain. I'm in my office trying to distract myself.

N: Poor baby :(

T: I was hoping you could help cheer me up.

N: Oh? And how would I do that?

T: Nudes.

N: Of course. I'm cleaning the apartment at the moment and I look like shit.

T: Come on, babe. Help a guy out.

N: Hmm.

There was a long pause and he started to get anxious.

T: You still there?

N: Hang on.

He bounced his knee and kept his eyes glued to the screen of his phone. Sixty seconds passed and he fought the urge to send another message. Ninety seconds. As he picked up the phone to type, a picture appeared. It was a selfie of her standing in the bathroom with her back to the mirror. She was wearing a red lace bra and matching panties. Her reflection in the mirror revealed that they were thong underwear. Thomas let out a whispered, "Yes," and instinctively checked over his shoulder before holding his phone up a little higher so he could get a better look. He tapped the image on his screen and downloaded it to a secret folder on his phone where he kept such treasures.

T: So hot!

He stood up and dropped his pants to the floor and sent her a dick pic. He sat back down to wait for her reply, which he hoped would bring with it something nude.

N: I see you're excited about something. Was it my pic or the porn I can see in the background on your computer?

He looked at the photograph he sent and sure enough, just in the background behind his dick was his computer screen, still freeze-framed on a hot blonde who was taking care of herself while lying on a bed with black satin sheets. He took another one with his junk facing the other direction and sent it to her.

T: I wasn't sure you were around or if you'd comply with my request so I had a backup plan going.

N: Mhmm.

T: Send me more. Same pose but no bra or panties.

There was another pause before her reply came through. This time he only had to wait thirty seconds and it was definitely worth it.

N: Something like this?

She was in the exact same pose, but fully nude.

T: Yeah, something like that. Now make your way to the bed.

N: Okay, now what?

T: Now hold the phone at arm's length above you and grab your breast with your other hand.

A few seconds passed and much to his delight, the photo came through.

T: Mmm. Excellent. Now a similar pose, but instead spread your legs and center the camera lower.

N: That's awfully dirty, Thomas.

T: Do it.

There was another long pause. After what felt like the longest two minutes of his life the photograph finally came through, only her free hand was between her spread legs, covering herself up.

T: Hey now, that's not what I meant!

N: Well, it's what you got.

T: Move your hand.

N: I'll see what I can do.

Another thirty seconds passed, and instead of a photograph, a disappointing text message came back.

N: My mother just called. I have to go.

T: Call her back later.

N: Seriously? What would you say if I said that to you?

T: That's different.

N: No, it's not different. Chat later. Bye.

He waited a full two minutes to see if another message was forthcoming, but it was not. He nibbled on his dinner, mostly shuffling the food around on his plate and shovelling the occasional bite into his mouth. She made up her mind and he wouldn't be continuing his naughty shenanigans. He put down his plate and redirected his attention to his computer screen.

SUNDAY, JULY 9, 8:00 P.M.

Thomas walked into his mother's room mumbling. "Am I the only one who hasn't lost his mind?" She looked alert as he approached and he pulled up a chair beside her bed. "Good evening, Mother, how are you feeling?"

She gave him a nod and a smile. She would understand his troubles but he decided not to bother her with them. Sitting by her bedside was the one thing that kept his blood pressure down. Brenda once asked him why he spent so much time doting on her while he ignored all the other people in the house. His response was simple. She gave him life and supported him throughout it. While everyone else took and took, she spent her life giving. If ever asked to pinpoint the exact moment he knew that he and his wife were no longer in love, the instant he uttered those words would be it.

He gently rubbed his mother's forehead and leaned in so she could hear him over the whoosh and whir of the machines helping keep her alive. "Would you like some cereal, mother?" A nod. "With a little brown sugar in it this time?" Another nod accompanied by a smile. "Okay then, give me a few minutes and I'll be right back."

Thomas walked to the kitchen, got out the Pablum, and filled a bowl with several scoops and some hot water, sprinkling a bit of brown sugar on top before giving it a stir.

Thomas fed his mother just as he did almost every evening. Small scoops of soft, mushy, warm food in between chin wipes and gentle pats on the head. If she started to get tired, which was often, he read to her until she fell asleep. There were only two spoonfuls of cereal left in the bowl but she couldn't take any more. "Would you like me to read to you?" A nod. "What shall we read today?" She looked towards the night side table, as she did every night, where there was always a book. Dickens was still there and the bookmark still in its place. He opened the book to where the marker was and started to read. She furrowed her brow and shook her head side to side. "What's the matter, mother? Would you rather I read you another book?"

She shook her head and motioned toward her breathing mask. He lifted it up and she managed a single raspy word. "Start."

"Start? As in, from the start? The beginning of the book?" A nod. Thomas turned to the front of the book and began to read, *"It was the best of times, it was the worst of times—"*

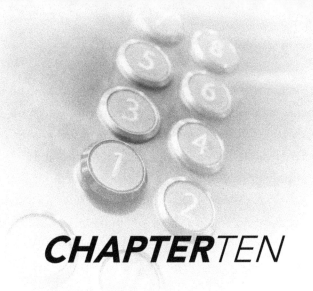

CHAPTER*TEN*

MONDAY, JULY 10, 7:00 A.M.

Thomas opened his eyes and immediately realized he had to move delicately. Sleeping in a chair slumped over with his face mushed against the side of a bed introduced more than one kink in his lower back and neck, and that was not counting his actual neck, which was just one big knot at that point. He sat up, tentative at first and then made his movements more pronounced as he stretched his arms and got his spine more or less back to its optimal position. Forgetting he was still wearing his watch, he looked around the room for a clock. There was an old cuckoo clock on the wall but it read seven o'clock. He was certain he had not checked the time on the clock or wound it in weeks so he figured the time on it was incorrect. Standing up, he reached high above his head to stretch and saw the watch on his wrist. Shaking his head at his own idiocy he checked the time. Seven o'clock. His mother was still sleeping so he tiptoed out of the room and closed the door.

Walking around the corner, he noticed that everything was pretty much in the same state as it was the night before. He called out down the hall. "Brenda? Brittany?" Then he remembered that Brittany had thrown a hissy fit and went to stay at a friend's place. But where was his wife? "Brenda?" There was no response. He walked to the bedroom and it was obvious that no one had slept there last night. Marching into the en suite, he checked her toothbrush. Dry.

He stared at himself in the mirror. "What the hell?" Grabbing his cell phone out of his pocket, he called Brenda. It went straight to voicemail.

"Hi, you've reached Brenda's voicemail. Please leave me a message. Toodles!"

"Bren, where the hell are you? Call me back, immediately." He hung up and called Brittany's cell phone next. It rang several times before it went to voicemail. "Brit, it's your father. I know you're screening your calls but I can't find your mother. Do you know where she might be? If you're with her just send me a text." Putting the phone down beside the sink, he leaned on the counter with both hands and pursed his lips. "Fuck it." He picked up his phone again and dialed Nikki. She picked up after the fourth ring and was still asleep.

"Hello?"

"Nik, it's Thomas."

"Thomas, it's... it's... it's only seven o'clock. You know I'm not a morning person, what is it? Is everything okay?"

Thomas considered telling her what was going on at home but decided against it. The whole point in having a mistress was to leave all those problems behind and just have some fun. "Uh, yeah, everything's fine. Listen, how would you like to come to the bank with me today? We'll get the security folks used to seeing you in there."

"More safety deposit box sexy times?"

"Wear a nice skirt just in case—panties optional."

"I only have nice things, Thomas, you know that. I'll be ready. I'll wait downstairs for you so you don't have to park."

Thomas checked his teeth in the mirror. "See you in a little bit. I have to wait for the nurse to show up." He turned his wrist and glanced down at his gold watch. "Should be within the hour."

"Okay, hun, I'll see you soon. Oh, and about last night. I'm really sorry. My mom was having a full-fledged panic attack and I couldn't leave her hanging."

"It's okay. You'll make it up to me at the bank," and without waiting for any more response he ended the call, walked into the kitchen, prepared himself a piping hot coffee, and waited for the home care nurse to show up for her shift.

MONDAY, JULY 10, 7:05 A.M.

Nikki turned to her overnight companion. "Get the fuck out. I'm going to assume he's showing up here an hour fucking early."

"Then that means we've got almost a whole hour." He put his hand on the back of her neck and leaned in for a kiss.

"Mitch! Get the fuck out. If you're not at the desk when he comes downstairs he'll get you fired."

"Jesus. Fine. I don't even start my shift until nine o'clock, though. This guy better be worth it. I'm getting tired of losing to him at poker and letting him screw you whenever he wants."

Nikki pushed him out of bed. "We'll address that 'letting him screw you' comment another time. For now, you have to go. And he's worth it. I'll tell you all about it when I get back." She kissed him on the forehead. "I'm hopping in the shower. You better be gone by the time I get out. I don't have to tell you how much hell will break loose if he shows up when you're here. Forget about money, you'll be lucky if they'll be able to identify your body at the morgue."

"Melodramatic much?"

"For two years I've been sleeping with this guy looking for a payday. I'm probably weeks away from realizing it. Don't mess this up for me, Mitch. I love you, I really do, but get the hell out."

—

Nikki managed to get herself dressed, fed, and downstairs to the foyer of her building with twenty minutes to spare. She pulled off looking elegant in her summer dress and heels without overdressing for a Monday morning. She waited five minutes and then saw Thomas's car pull up in front and come to a stop between the two *No Stopping* signs in front of her building. He honked the horn before she could even approach the door. Nikki got into the car and he was already talking, leaving a message for someone.

"So you can go in if you want or have things to do or you can have the day off. It's up to you. I'll see you tomorrow."

Nikki leaned over and gave him a kiss. "Not going into work today?"

"Nah. I'm just not feeling up to it. I'd rather have a bit of fun. Are you ready to go see a shit ton of money again?"

"Yes please! I love it when you talk dirty. Say it again."

"Shit ton of money."

"It sounds so, I don't know, big, but it took up a lot less room than I thought it would."

Thomas couldn't help but chuckle. "If you counted it off in singles it would look big. I'm used to seeing big bills all in one spot so it's not surprising to me. If you didn't see that all the time I can see how there'd be no frame of reference. Just to give you an idea of scale, if I were to have the bank convert all my used bills into fresh, brand new fifties and hundreds, all the money I have in cash would easily fit in a suitcase."

"New or old matters?"

"For sure. Old bills are thicker because the paper wears, creases, and in some cases tears. Canada has less of a problem with this now that their bills are made of this polymer."

"I heard they were waterproof and the hundred smells like maple syrup."

"Heh. Well, one of those two things is likely true. I'll let you figure out which one. For us, the Federal Reserve issues bills of all denomination in hundred bill straps and four thousand bill bricks. If I converted all my money into hundred-dollar straps that would be ten thousand dollars per strap and it's less than half an inch thick." He held up his hands with thumb and index finger roughly half an inch apart. "Just for fun let's say I got some fifty dollar straps as well, so those are five grand a piece and I would need two to total ten grand so they'd be about an inch think. You with me so far?" Nikki nodded and he continued his money math lesson. "Right, so let's say that I have most of the money in hundreds and a couple hundred thousand in fifties. I would need a hundred and sixty straps of hundreds and forty bundles of fifties. That's one hundred inches thick if I lay them on top of each other like a giant tower. Much too tall, right?"

"For sure, that'd be almost eight feet high."

"But—" he held up one finger, "— but, make it five stacks wide and four stacks long? That's only ten straps deep. Five inches. You could pack it in a big suitcase and have clothes on top and underneath, with room to spare."

Nikki slouched.

"What's the matter babe?"

"I dunno, I guess I was somehow hoping it would look like a lot more money."

"This isn't a cartoon, honey, and I ain't Scrooge McDuck. Plus, money is money. It still spends the same. This reminds me, I bought you something, but it's being delivered so I can't give it to you until later today."

"Tease."

He gave her a wink and parked the car a block down from the bank.

"Why aren't you parking in front? It looked like there were spots?"

"Ever since the last attempts at robbing a couple of the downtown branches they've banned parking in front of the bank entrance."

"What, like there are still people with getaway cars hanging out front waiting for the bag man to come out and throw the loot through the open back window, get in the front and say, 'Step on it!'?"

He let out a booming laugh. She was one of the only people in the world that could make him laugh so freely. "Yeah, something like that." The two walked toward the bank and a few yards away he stopped. He took the key off his keyring and handed it to her. "Okay, let's test the bank's procedures. You should have no problem getting in. Do you have your ID?"

"Yep."

"Do you remember your PIN?"

"Yep." She leaned over and added with a whisper, "It's your birthday."

"That's very sweet of you. Now, walk in there with the attitude that you own the place, go down to my box, and take it to a viewing room. I'll meet you in there." He lit a cigarette and gave her a pat on the bum. She took a deep breath and walked towards the bank, up the stairs, and into the front door.

—

Once inside, she walked across the marble floor, her heels click clacking like a mistress on a mission, and approached the same attendant that set up her access on Friday. "Good morning, I'd like to access my safety deposit box."

"Welcome back, Miss Carcillo. May I please see some identification?"

She handed him over her driver's license and he placed it in front of him beside his keyboard. He typed a few things, then held the identification up and compared the photo to the woman standing in front of him. "It's a terrible photo of me. How come the DMV can't seem to take a decent photo of anyone these days?"

"If it's any consolation, ma'am, the security photo we took of you the other day looks fantastic. You're as radiant as ever."

She felt her cheeks warm as he handed her back her identification. "I just punch in my PIN now?"

"Yes, that's correct."

She punched in one-one-two-one and a green light lit up above the keypad.

"Now, if you'll just come down with me I'll take you to your container."

As she did the first time, Nikki walked in awe of the magnificence of the bank's architecture. Marble was everywhere. Every handrail sparkled. Natural light shone in from stained glass windows as they made their way down the staircase. Even underground the building gave the appearance that there was sunlight. She looked around to see if there were any windows or skylights. There were not.

The attendant stood outside the vault-like room that housed the safety deposit boxes and extended his arm. "Here you go, ma'am."

"You forgot to give me a viewing room key."

"Oh, I'm terribly sorry, Miss Carcillo, here you go." He handed her the key to viewing room number two.

She entered the deposit box vault and slid the key into the lock. Pulling out the locker, which she found heavier than she expected, she plopped it down on top of a wheeled dolly. She made her way to viewing room number two and closed the door. Uncertain how long she should wait, she opened the locker and started to take bundles out and lay them on the table. At first she kept them neat and tidy, square to the edges of the table in the center of the room. After she lay several bundles flat, she stopped counting and just started dumping the money out onto the table, grabbing with both hands and tossing it into a pile in an effort to make to make it look bigger, so it would take up the amount of space she thought almost two million dollars should take.

She caught movement out of the corner of her eye. It was Thomas. "Jesus Christ on a cracker, Thomas, you scared the living shit out of me."

"Sorry, babe, but I didn't want to wait too long to join you. I was hoping you'd be down here for a little while. I see you're making a fort of some kind?"

She looked down at the pile of money. "I wanted to make it bigger."

"I'm not sure if you succeeded but you're making something else bigger."

He waggled his eyebrows and for the second time in the last ten minutes she felt her cheeks warm. He stepped in behind her, reached around, and spread the money across the table. Putting his hand on her back between her shoulder blades he bent her forward so her chest was on top of the cash. "Thomas, what are you doing?"

He lifted up her skirt and knelt down and pulled her underwear until it was sitting atop her feet on the ground. He lifted one of her feet and it slipped out of the leg hole in her lace boy-cut panties. Standing up, he pushed her down on the table and entered her from behind. He held her there as he continued to do as he pleased. She held the table top in a giant bear hug with her arms wide and over a million dollars pressed against her chest. He finished with a loud grunt and stepped away. With piles of money strewn across the floor she panted and clutched several bundles that had not managed to escape in her hands. He bent down and guided her foot through the leg opening in her underwear and pulled them up and back into their rightful spot.

"Now how about you help me clean up this mess. If you do a good job you can slide one of those strips into your purse." He looked over at the empty locker on the trolley, took the key out of the lock, and put it back on his keychain before returning the keys to his pocket and helping her pick up the cash and put it all back into the locker. As he started to shut the lid she snuck her hand in, pulled out a bundle, and kissed him on the nose.

Back at the car, he looked over at her with a smile. "You know, I was looking at islands last night."

"Oh?"

"Yep. Would you prefer the South Pacific or the Caribbean?"

"Oooooh, I have choices! I'll have to think about it."

"You do that. I'm not sure what I'll do. It won't be the office."

She flashed her bundle of cash. "I think I'm going to go shopping."

"As you wish m'dear. Where'd you like to go? I think I'll go golfing. I can drop you wherever though."

"Just drop me at the subway. I can get where I need to go from there and then grab an Uber."

Thomas drove her to the nearest subway stop and waved goodbye before cutting into traffic to a cacophony of screeching tires, car horns, and yelling.

CHAPTERELEVEN

The revolving door at the front entrance started to rotate and Nikki ducked under the security desk as a girl walked into the foyer. It was Brittany. She glanced over in Mitch's direction and headed for the west stairwell.

Thomas checked his watch. It had been twenty-five minutes since the power went out. He followed her movements up each floor on the camera. His anxiety started to subside with each step she took toward the top. When she got to in between the fifth and sixth floors she stopped and checked her watch. Thomas started to yell. "Why are you stopping? Why the fuck are you stopping?" He looked at the camera he had fixed on the lobby. Nikki was standing beside Mitch again but the changing reflection of the sun off the revolving door sent her diving back under the counter again. It was Mike and a tall black man. He brought his face closer to the monitor and squinted. It was Jay.

Mike ordered Jay to stand over by the front door and he walked over to Mitch who was sitting behind the desk and nervously fidgeting. "Power's out, eh?"

"Yeah, you'll have to walk up the stairs to see Thom—uh, Mr. Van Steen, and I'll need you to sign in."

Mike put his hands on the desk. In one he was holding a wad of bills. It was nowhere near what Nikki had brought him earlier, but it was still enough to get his attention.

"I was hoping we could avoid a log entry today, if it's all the same with you."

Mike peeled off two bills and placed them on the desk. Mitch took the cash. Mike looked around and then pointed to the panel of security camera monitors in front of Mitch. "How long is that stored for?"

Mitch shrugged. "I don't know to be honest. I think it only records when it detects motion and is set to only record to a certain file size."

Mike peeled off two more bills and placed them on the counter. "Any chance you can turn off the fifth floor recording until I get back?"

Mitch looked over at Jay, then back to Mike, and then down at the cash on the counter. "Maybe." Mike nodded and handed him another bill. He took it and then typed for a few seconds, pressing his last keystroke with great emphasis. "Okay, five's cold until you tell me otherwise or I see you leave."

"Thanks, Mitch. I knew you weren't such a bad guy. One more thing, and I'm hoping this one won't cost me anything. Can you just turn off these monitors here for a bit? I'm going to want some privacy." Mitch flipped the switch on each of the monitors and the screens went dark. Mike nodded and motioned to Jay and the two walked over to the stairwell. Thomas was glued to the monitor and fully aware that it was not recording.

"Brittany, change floors! Keep walking and change floors! Fuck!"

*PART*THREE

MIKE & BRITTANY

CHAPTER*TWELVE*

With the ink still drying on the contract with Stephen, Thomas took the remainder of the afternoon off. Figuring it could only pay off in sex from Jenny in the near future, he gave her the rest of the afternoon off as well. He slipped three hundred dollar bills into her hand before he gave her ass a squeeze on his way out the door. "Go buy something pretty to wear under your outfit for Monday morning."

Jenny leaned forward, gave Thomas a healthy look at her breasts, and planted a kiss on his cheek as she took the money. "Of course. Black, white, or red?"

"Surprise me."

With the afternoon at his disposal, he headed over to one of his rental properties to check in on his friend, Mike. He pressed the Bluetooth connect button on the steering wheel of his Audi TT. The slightly feminine but noticeably computer-generated voice of his car's communication system sprung to life.

"Who would you like to call?"

His car had a habit of never getting Mike's name right, no matter how he entered the correct name into the system. Recent voice-dialing debacles saw his car attempt to call "Mister T."

"Call Mikey Vee."

"Calling Mikey Vee."

Thomas muttered into his steering wheel. "Stupid car finally got it right. For what I paid for you, you should've been getting that right a long time ago."

On the third ring, Mike picked up the phone. *"Ha-low. Mike speakin'."*

"Mike, it's Tommy."

"Oh, hey, buddy. To what do I owe the pleasure on this beautiful Friday? If you're looking for a little afternoon delight then I gotta tell ya up front, I'm not in the mood for oral."

"Jesus Christ, man, are you high?"

"Only a little."

"What have I told you about getting high when you're working? How are the addicts in the building going to respect you if you keep sinking down to their level? You're the building manager for Christ's sake. The building manager in my building, I might add."

"Dude, just chillax. Seriously. I don't do that shit. None of it, man. No smack, no crack, no meth. My only love is Mary Jane. A couple hits off the trusty bong just to take the edge off. I was up all night with the cops causing a ruckus down the hall."

"Jesus, and you thought that throwing on some Bob Marley and lighting up was the best idea you've ever had? I know it was only community college, Mikey, but how did you not flunk out?"

"Blow jobs, Tommy. Lots and lots of blow jobs."

"You're an idiot, you know that? Put some pants on, I'm almost there." Thomas heard some rustling, the sound of a lighter flicking, and the tell-tale bubbling that came with someone taking a big hit off a bong. "And for crying out loud, stop smoking and open a window. I can't go to Nikki's smelling like an extra from a stoner movie."

Thomas hung up and fished a cigarette out of his briefcase. He almost swerved into oncoming traffic as he tried to find his monogrammed Zippo amongst all the papers and candy bar wrappers in his briefcase. He lit a Camel Light and tossed the lighter onto the passenger seat, rolled down his window, and put both hands back on the steering wheel in an effort to slow down his heart rate, which skipped two solid beats after his near death experience crossing the yellow line on one of the busiest city streets in the world.

Pulling up to the front of the five-story, thirty-unit apartment complex, he parked illegally in front of the building. He hadn't seen a police car within a mile of the place since he bought it five years ago, so the illegality of his parking job was the least of his concerns. If what Mike said were true, the cops were stopping by all the time, though. The rent was cheap and while not officially designated as a crack house, the tenants were not exactly shopping on Fifth Avenue. In fact, Thomas would bet cold, hard cash that anything valuable they owned came with a five-finger discount.

The front door to the building gave the impression that it might be secure, but it wasn't. The buzzer hadn't worked in almost a year and the security camera was just for show. Every once in a while Thomas would replace the battery in the camera housing that kept the little red LED light flashing—and everyone convinced that it was plugged into something and recording. Even still, with the steady stream of cops in and out of the complex it didn't appear to have much of a deterrent on some of the tenants. He didn't visit often but found that the only saving grace was all the dealers and addicts kept to themselves. Thomas knocked on the door with a makeshift *"Building Manager"* sign taped over top of the rusted 1A plaque just below the peephole.

"Come in!"

Mike's voice never sounded too far away from the door. Thomas opened it and the smell of marijuana hit him square in the face. "Jesus Christ on a cracker, Mike. I could have been police. You're ten feet from the door. Would it have killed you to just get up and check on who it was before just inviting them in?"

Mike sat on his floral print couch circa 1974 in a white sleeveless t-shirt and a pair of red boxer briefs with *"IN CASE OF EMERGENCY PULL DOWN"* printed on the front. "Easy man, I saw your car pull up out front."

"From the couch? You can't even see the window!"

Mike waved him over. He walked to the couch and leaned in the direction Mike was pointing.

"What the…?"

An intricate system of several cheap flea market mirrors were strategically positioned around the apartment. Some were propped up on chairs and others were hung on doors. There was even one duct-taped to the front of a rotating fan and a metal medicine cabinet bolted to a cupboard door in the kitchen.

"I fixed the security system."

Thomas plopped down on the couch beside Mike and picked up the bong and dollar-store lighter from the coffee table. Flicking the Bic, he held the flame to the glass bowl and inhaled. Holding his breath, he turned to Mike and short puffs of smoke slipped out from between his lips as he mumbled.

"You're an idiot. You know that?" He sat in silence and waited for the buzz to kick in, which didn't take long. "Dude, where did you get this weed?"

"I know, right? It's the most intense stuff I've ever had, but at the same time the most mellow."

"Seriously, where did you get it?"

"Why, do you want some? I can hook you up if you're looking to keep a small stash on hand for emergencies." He attempted to air quote "emergencies" but missed by half a beat. "It's way better for you than those damn cigarettes you smoke, that's for damn sure."

"I don't smoke."

"Holy shit, man, denial isn't just a river in, you know, the Middle East or some shit."

Thomas raised his hand to swat at him. "Just tell me where you got the weed before I smack you upside the head, all right?"

Mike blocked his face with his arms and retreated to the corner of the couch. "Okay. Okay. Jesus. I guess your body doesn't pull the mellow out of this stuff like it does for normal people. You have to relax, man."

Thomas lowered his hand, turned his head sideways with calm deliberation, and released a loud pop as his neck cracked. Mike made his best "that's gotta hurt" face and mouthed the word "ouch." Thomas put his hands in his lap, relaxed his shoulders, and gazed toward the window behind the sofa.

"I really liked the weed, Mikey. Would you please be so kind as to provide me with information as to how you came into possession of this fine herb so that I can go about obtaining some for my own personal enjoyment when I feel it is appropriate to do so?"

"Yeah, sure man. No problem. Was that so hard? Geez."

He got up off the couch and meandered over to the not-quite-fully-assembled desk in the corner of the room. He rummaged through some bills and random scraps of paper until he found the one he was looking for. "Here man, call this number and ask for Johnny Christmas."

He took the slip of paper and raised an eyebrow. "Johnny Christmas?"

"That's the name I was given. He's from Canada. Way out in B.C. where the skiing is cool and the girls are—uh—polite. Since Canadians own the North Pole and shit you can think of him as the Santa Claus of marijuana."

"How does he get it across the border?"

"How the hell would I know? Under no uncertain terms do I want to know, nor do I give a single fuck about it. Not one. I have no fucks to give on this subject. None. Zero."

"All right, all right, I get your point. Jesus, take another hit and calm down. Can I keep this?" He held up the slip of paper.

"Negatory, my good friend." Mike burped between tokes from his bong. "Too many years of smoking this stuff and I'm lucky if I can remember if I ate lunch. Put the number in your fancy phone or something."

"Why don't you put it in your phone, Mike? Then you won't have to remember where you put the little slip of paper?"

"Dude, I have a land line and I almost never leave the apartment except to deal with a bullshit tenant or to go get groceries. Why the hell would I need a cell phone? Plus, you don't pay me enough to enjoy such luxuries."

"You ungrateful shit. I pay you more than enough to keep this rat-hole building from being condemned, and it's more than you deserve, you lazy bastard." He actually smacked him in the head, although not nearly as hard as he wanted to.

"Me? Lazy? Coming from the dude who dropped out of the same college I did only to come into a small seven-figure loan from daddy?"

Thomas jumped up off the couch and pointed a finger him. "You leave my father out of this!"

Mike raised his hands in apology. "You're right, dude. You're right. I'm sorry, that was offside."

Thomas sat back down on the couch. "Damn right it was. Look, you fucking reek and I'm starting to smell, too. Let's head out and see if we can't get in a game of pick-up ball. We haven't shot hoops in for fucking ever."

Mike looked over at Thomas and then down at his legs. "I suppose this requires pants."

Thomas let out a long sigh before getting off the couch. He walked to Mike's room and rummaged through his drawers until he found a t-shirt and pair of sport shorts. On his way to the kitchen, he threw the clothes at him. "Where can I get a glass?"

Through the fabric of the t-shirt partially over his head, he called out. "Medicine cabinet!"

Thomas looked at the kitchen serving at least partially as a do-it-yourself spy operation. "In the medicine cabinet, or in the cabinet that the medicine cabinet is bolted to?"

"The cabinet, cabinet. Dude, putting glassware in the medicine cabinet is just irresponsible."

Thomas rolled his eyes. "Yes, what was I thinking? Get dressed, dumbass, I gotta let off some steam before I go see Nikki. She doesn't like it when I'm all edgy. She likes sex to be all Zen and shit."

Mike got up off the couch, grabbed his sneakers, and slid into a pair of black flip-flops. "You're still seeing her on the side, eh?"

Thomas left his glass on the counter and quickly peeked to see if Mike was paying any attention. When he saw that he wasn't, he took a glass from the cabinet and put it in the medicine cabinet before joining Mike by the door. "Yeah. I mean, wouldn't you?"

"For sure, dude, she's fucking hot." He closed the door and headed toward the foyer.

"Are you going to lock that, or what?"

Mike looked over his shoulder as he pulled on the handle to the building door. "Have you seen my apartment? Taking shit out of there would be a vast improvement."

Thomas shook his head. "What're you doing with all the money I'm paying you?"

"401K."

"Are you shitting me? All your money is going into your retirement fund?"

He kept walking, a decided spring in his step since he left the building. "Yup. Saving up enough so I can get my ass to an island where I can just lay on the beach without a care in the world."

Thomas opened the door to the gym and held it open. "As opposed to now, where the day-to-day grind is just wearing you down?"

"Very funny. I have responsibilities here. I have to keep your sorry ass out of slumlord jail, or wherever it is they toss guys like you when your buildings go to shit. Plus, the weather here sucks."

The pair changed quickly and headed into the gym where a game of basketball was already underway. It looked like a little 3-on-3, with room for more, so while limbering up Thomas got the attention of one of the guys on court.

"We good here?" His tone indicated that it wasn't a request so much as it was a statement.

A tall, solid-looking black guy easily fifteen years Thomas's junior pointed at Mike. "We'll take the less fat guy."

Thomas held his arms out, palms up in protest. "Hey, I'm clearly taller!"

His protest fell on deaf ears and to add insult to injury another player chimed in. "Yeah, but you fat."

"Oh, it's going to be like that, is it?" The player who made the fat comment stopped playing and walked over to Thomas, standing tall with his head held high and his chest puffed out, almost touching his.

"It's not just gonna be like that, not short fat man. It's how it is."

Mike shot a glance over at Thomas that screamed, "Don't go there." Thomas took a confident step to the side and hopped onto the court. It took the big mouth and Mike a couple beats to realize their team was all of a sudden playing two against four, so they jumped in and joined the play. The game was rough and didn't so much have the feel of a friendly pick-up game as it did an MMA training session. Thomas was easily the biggest, whitest, clumsiest fish out of water in the whole gym, with Mike a close second.

Thomas took an in-bound pass from one of his teammates and streaked down the court, showing a brief glimpse of the athlete he once was. He drove toward the net and the guy from his almost-sideline altercation stepped in front of him, stuffing his shoulder right into the center of Thomas's chest, sending him to the hardwood, and releasing all the air from his lungs.

"What's the matter, big and tall? You think you been fouled?" He raised his arm with a closed fist and started to take a swing at Thomas.

Mike rushed in and tackled him and the two bounced out of bounds. Mike put his hand on his chest and cocked his head to one side. "I think we're done playing now, Jay. You hear me, Capital Jay? We're done here. Is that all right?"

He looked up and briefly considered making something more out of it but Mike widened his eyes and gave his head the nod.

"Yeah, it's all right, Mikey Vee."

"Perfect."

"Let's get Tommy up off his ass here and we'll get out of your way."

They both extended a hand to Thomas and helped him up from the floor. His head jerked back and forth between the two. Jay shrugged his shoulders and Mike put his arm around Thomas and walked him toward the locker room.

"I'll tell you later." Looking back over his shoulder he added, "Thanks for the game, guys." The game had already resumed and they might have well been invisible.

In the locker room, Thomas couldn't get the connection between Jay and Mike off his mind. "Dude, you know that asshole? Why didn't you say you knew him?"

Mike looked around, eyes shifting from side to side. He checked around the corner and Thomas spun him around by the shoulder.

"Dude, what the fuck? What's with all the paranoia? This is why you shouldn't be smoking that stuff all the time, man. It's making you all weird."

"It's complicated."

"What are you, describing your latest relationship to all your friends on Facebook? How is it fucking complicated? You know him. He knows you. He's a giant asshole, probably a drug dealer, likely destined for prison if he hasn't already been. You? Well, I'm pretty sure you're two of those things but that's where the similarities end."

Mike gave him the finger. "Two A."

"What?"

He repeated himself, with a little more emphasis. "Two. A."

His eyes widened.

"Ohhhhhhh. Two fucking A? In your building? Are you shitting me?"

"Lower your voice man, motherfucker has people everywhere, and none of them are gonna stop and help you change a flat tire, if you know what I mean."

He brought his voice down to a whisper. "I thought the building was just filled with lowlife down-on-your-luck loser types. Domestic abusers and addicts. Is that what that dude is dealing? What the actual fuck? I am sure I can get him evicted if it'll make your life easier."

"No fucking way, man. That will make my life the opposite of easier. That place is just the one he has on the books. He doesn't deal out of that apartment but I'm sure he uses it for less than morally upstanding behaviour, not the least of which is banging a few dozen women every week."

"Sounds charming."

"He's actually not a bad tenant, if I'm being completely honest. He keeps his place clean, doesn't smoke inside—always kicking people out on the fire escape when they want to light up, and until last night hasn't even attracted the least bit of attention."

"And what happened last night?"

"Some junkie followed him back. Security being what it is the dude just wandered up and knocked on his door, apparently just as he was shimmying a pair of panties down this girl's legs. I'm actually surprised he didn't put a cap in the dude right there in the hallway. Anyway, lots of yelling, lots of attempted murder slash 'self defense' and before you know it the cops are there and asking a lot of questions about what the fuck happened."

"Jesus. Anyone arrested? Charges?"

"No, sir. Jay talked his way out of it. Played the junkie as a junkie who was just misremembering. Cop was a brother, so Jay played if off as just crazy white."

"Cop doesn't have Jay pegged as a player? Or is he on the take?"

"Nah, Jay's pretty new to the game far as I can tell. Plus his honey house is in a piece of shit neighbourhood. If he was all that he'd have a place in the burbs and have a front that was better than the god dammed video store two blocks over. Seriously, Blockbuster couldn't make that shit work and he thinks the narcs, or even the dumb ass feds, are going to think he's legit?"

"Unless he's the number one or two player he is the least of their problems."

"Yeah, well anyway, dude's got more drugs to sell than he has brains, but the man can talk his way out of anything. No word of a lie, he should be in a legit sales job. He'd make as much money and not have the risk of getting killed or going to prison for forever."

"Fuck, man. How do you know all this?"

"I don't leave the fucking couch, man, and all the damn walls are paper thin. Plus, I get calls for all kinds of stuff and get to poke around in people's places looking for the circuit breaker or what-have-you. Oh, that reminds me. Jay's requested you fix the buzzer on the front door so people gotta get buzzed in."

"Goddammit, what's that going to cost me?"

"Dunno man, more than you wanna pay, I'm sure. But given he pays his rent on time, which is more than I can say for most of the deadbeats. I say we get it fixed. Who knows, maybe it'll attract a different class of tenant?"

"Fuck. All right, fine. Make some calls tomorrow and tell Jay I'll take care of it. But tell him I'm taking care of it, not you, and then you take care of it. I don't want to be on any gang banger list or anything."

"No worries, boss." He extended his fist to get a bump but there was no hint of reciprocation.

"I have to get my butt over to Nikki's and then get home to my pain in the ass wife. Thanks for the phone number."

"My pleasure. Tell him Mike sent you. He'll give you the good stuff."

*CHAPTER*THIRTEEN

Mike rolled over and his hand encountered another body. He opened one eye and saw a naked woman sleeping beside him. He ran through the events of the last twenty-four hours in his head and tried to figure out who she was and where she came from. He pulled the covers back and got a better look at her body. She was white, so she was not one of Jay's girls. She looked eighteen, so that was good news. She didn't look much older than eighteen, so that was a bit of a concern, but not one that he was going to lose any sleep over. She didn't appear to have any track marks on her arms and none anywhere else that he could see, at least. He inhaled for a count of six. The room smelled like a mixture of weed and sex. Still the best combination of any two things he could come up with, and slightly ahead of a nice Canadian rye whiskey and ginger ale. He slipped out of bed and peered into the garbage can on the other side of his night table. Inside he found three condom wrappers and two used condoms.

He turned and addressed the bedside lamp that was missing its shade. "Now that's weird."

He slid back into bed. The girl rolled over and her legs fell apart. Sticking out of her vagina was the end of the third condom. He turned back to the lamp, laughing. "No, that's hilarious." He reached between her legs and pulled out the rubber. From the look of things, it appeared he ran out of gas sometime during round three and the two of them passed out.

The girl stretched and yawned, opening her eyes just a crack, one at a time. Mike threw the condom over his shoulder in the general direction of the waste bin and put on his best casual smile as he propped himself up on his elbow. He couldn't come up with a name, so decided to try an old trick he learned in college before he dropped out. He extended his hand to the naked girl in his bed. "Hi, my name's Mike. What's yours?"

The girl's eyes widened and she scrambled to cover up with the blankets.

Mike laughed. "That's funny. Considering what I just pulled out of your vagina you'd think you wouldn't be so modest."

"You pulled *what* out of *where?*" She lifted the sheet up so she could peer down between her legs. Satisfied that there was no visible damage and feeling no pain she lowered the sheet and gave Mike a stern look. "Well?"

"Oh." He was trying to contain his laughter but did a poor job of it. "You actually wanted me to tell you. Well, all right—it, um—seems like uh—amidst—um, well, during what appears to be our third round of, uh—coitus we both passed out and I uh—left a prophylactic wedged in your vajayjay."

"Oh. My. God. I'm going to die. You left a condom in my pussy?"

"I think you're just as culpable here."

The girl raised her eyebrows.

"All I'm saying is it takes two to tango, and hey, look on the bright side. Your snatch is so tight it yanked the condom right off my dick!"

"Eww, and yeah, I'm like half your age—at least. You're probably used to old lady cooch that looks like a leather purse. How old are you anyway, and how high did I have to get to sleep with you more than once?"

"Considering the amount of weed I smoke I think I'm doing all right. I'm not sure how high you were but from the smell of us I'd say we were drinking. Jägermeister probably. You young chicks love to get shitfaced on that crap. And before you get any ideas I didn't slip you anything in your drink."

"I am well aware of what was in all my drinks and drugs, thank you very much, but why would you even think to say that? Ugh, seriously?"

"Which part, the Jägermeister bit, or the rufie bit?"

"Get me my clothes so I can leave, please."

"Geez, fine. Okay." He got up from the bed, still naked, and walked around picking up her clothes. He tossed them to her on the bed and turned around to go open a window, scratching his butt as he returned with an erection.

"Well would you look at that? You sure you don't wanna stick around for a bit? We can finish round three."

With everything but her shirt back on she made a run for the washroom to throw up. While bent over the toilet Mike leaned his head in through the doorway. "Yup, that'd be the Jäger talking. I'm going to say that you're taking a pass on more sex."

With her head still in the bowl, she flushed the toilet and gave him the finger.

"Gotcha. Well, there's an unopened spare toothbrush in the basket under the sink if you want to brush your teeth. I gotta hop in the shower so you can take your time there. Just give me a heads up if you're going to flush again."

Mike stepped over her as she prayed to the porcelain gods and hopped into the shower.

"Can I at least get your name?"

Flush. "No."

"Hey! Fuck! I told you to warn me! Look, I know you were at the same party I was at last night. You're friends with Brittany Van Steen."

She pulled the shower curtain back and he instinctively covered up. "No shit, Sherlock. You're her dealer. Why do you think I picked you?"

Mike raised his hands in defense. "Hey, now, no, no, no, nooooooo. I just know her dad. He owns this place and I manage it for him. What do you mean you picked me?"

"I just slept with my friend's dad's friend in a sleazy apartment, twice, and had his condom stuck in my vagina for several hours while he probably slept and farted and scratched himself. There isn't enough bleach in New York City to wipe that memory from my brain. Look, a girl's got to drink and smoke for free somehow. I have better shit to spend my money on."

"Hey now, no need to be rude about it! Look, I won't tell anyone if you don't tell anyone."

She spat into the sink, rinsed her mouth, and tried to touch up her hair a bit before giving up and putting it back into a ponytail. "I can guarantee you I'm not telling anyone."

He rinsed the shampoo out of his hair. "Well, all right then. It'll just be our little secret. Help yourself to anything you want in the kitchen, I'm going to take care of something in here for a bit."

"Disgusting." She flushed the toilet again and left the bathroom.

Mike toweled off and looked around the apartment for his bong. He normally left it on the coffee table but for some reason his stuff wasn't where it was supposed to be. He must have been trying to impress the girl, who, based on her recent revelation, didn't require impressing. Mike found it beside the bed along with a pair of women's thong underwear poking out from the faded bed skirt. He turned on the switch to his night side table lamp that was missing the shade.

He put a morsel of weed in the bowl of his bong, lit it up, and took a good long haul. Picking up his phone, he dialled Brittany.

She answered on the first ring. *"Yeah?"*

"Brit, it's Mike."

"Yeah, I have call display and you're in my contacts. Why are you calling me? I'm on my way home. I could have been there."

"I figured you were still at the after party. Last thing I remember you were getting your groove on pretty spectacularly with that brunette in the heels."

"Thought I'd give you a little spank material before bed. Ass. What do you want?"

"No need for the attitude, little missy. Need I remind you of our arrangement?"

"Since I'm the one who came up with the arrangement I can safely say I don't need reminding."

"Holy hell, you and your friends are pieces of work. Speaking of which, who is your friend? The blonde who was wearing the tight girl cut grey Yankees shirt with the blue jeans and the a-plus ass?"

"Yankees shirt? That would be Melissa. Why? Did she come up short on her arrangement or something?"

"Next time you see her you can tell her that she left her underwear at my apartment." Mike barely finished the sentence without giggling.

"Are you for real, Mike?"

"What can I say? The ladies find me irresistible. Are you jealous?"

"Jealous? No, I am not jealous. I'm proud of my friend for employing similar tactics to mine. I'm also disappointed in you, though if I think about it, I can't say I'm surprised. You have a weak spot when it comes to women of a certain persuasion."

"You talk a lot. Look, we both just got really drunk and ended up back at my place. I even shared my bong, and you know how protective I am of it. Then we had sex two and a half times and passed out."

"I'm well aware of your uncanny and sometimes inappropriate relationship you have with your bong. Wait, what? Two and a half?"

"Yeah, it's a long story. You should ask her about it next time you see her. Look, she's probably not going to want to come back here. If she wants her underpants I can give 'em to you next time I see you."

"Mike, you're a disgusting pervert, you know that?"

"I don't have it in writing from anyone yet but I'm starting to get the feeling that's what people think."

"It's not what people think, Mike, it's what they know, and I can speak on behalf of Melissa and tell you that you can keep her underwear. Consider it part of the payment for goods provided and services rendered."

"Ouch. Okay then. Don't forget our deal, girlie. Remember, I know where you live."

"Yeah, yeah. Okay. Jesus. Look I'm almost home, I gotta run. Is there anything else?"

"Nah, I think that's it for now. Toodles!" Mike paused waiting for a response but she hung up without saying another word. He looked over at the underpants hanging off the switch on his nightstand lamp and took another long haul off his bong. Wandering around to his side of the bed, he checked for his wallet. It was sticking out of the back pocket of his faded jeans on the floor. Empty. He let out long sigh as the smoke from his lungs drifted out of the open window.

SATURDAY, JULY 8, 12:00 P.M.

In the middle of his toke, Mike's phone rang and the familiar tone of MC Hammer's "Can't Touch This" echoed throughout his bedroom. "Y'allo!"

Jay's voice on the other end of the line was chipper. *"Hey, man, we gotta do the rounds today. You wanna start at your place or end up there?"*

Mike pondered this for a moment, waiting for his weed to kick in. "Aw man, had you asked me five minutes ago I most certainly would have said end here, but I'm a couple tokes into it here and the inertia is powerful."

"Shit, dude, you aren't making me do the rounds on my own again."

"Um…."

"That's bullshit. Get up off your white high-as-fuck fat ass and get over to the 86th Street Hustle. I'll meet you out front. Fifteen minutes! Don't be late, motherfucker."

Mike took another hit. "You seem agitated."

"Oh, do I? I wonder why that is? Just put some damn clothes on and get your ass down here. Fuck, this supposed to be less of a pain in the ass than a fucking real job."

Mike pulled on a pair of pants and an Aerosmith t-shirt. "Life is full of surprises, man. I'm dressed and heading out the door. Don't make me wait."

"You mother—" Mike hung up before he could finish his sentence.

Mike arrived at the 86th Street Hustle a couple seconds after Jay. They fist bumped and looked around for any cops or other unusual activity. Mike was the building manager for six of Thomas's buildings. He lived in one and kept the superintendent's apartment available in the other five for one of Jay's guys to use to run his business. The two walked up the front steps and knocked on the super's door. The sound of footsteps travelled across the apartment floor but there was no shadow of feet standing near the door. A voice came from further into the apartment.

"Jay, Mike. What's the word?"

"Let us in."

The door made a click sound and the two opened it, walked in, and then took an immediate left. The main bedroom had a steel-reinforced door and metal along all the outside walls, the walls shared with other rooms, and the ceiling. Metal even covered the window. It was less like a bedroom than it was a vault—or a big, metal coffin.

Jay gave the tall skinny black man a fist bump and Mike a nod. Jay walked over to the safe sitting in the corner, which was already open, and took out several bundles of cash and put them into a gym bag. He covered the money with a t-shirt and pair of shorts and a small toiletry bag. The two black men fist bumped again and Mike gave another nod as he and Jay exited the room and went down to the car.

Mike turned to Jay on the way to their cars. "I wasn't paying attention when you were packing. Look okay?"

Jay pondered the weight of the gym bag in his hand for a few moments, lifting it and lowering it as he walked down the front steps to the building. "Yeah, seems like it. Won't know until we get home and count it but it feels good. Maybe even a bit heavy, which is nice."

"Well if that's the case make sure to spread the love, okay? These guys need to be rewarded for going above and beyond."

"Yeah, man. Word. Since we're on the topic and all didn't you and that chick, Brittany's friend have an 'above and beyond' moment last night?"

"Shit, yeah. I almost forgot to tell you about that."

"Did she put out or pass out?"

He threw the gym bag in the back of his car and stood near the rear of the vehicle playing with his keys waiting for him to respond.

"A little bit from Column A and a little bit from Column B, and I'm not entirely sure she didn't slip something in my drink? Because I am real foggy on a lot of the details."

Jay shrugged his shoulders. "It's entirely possible. That party was lit. Plus, you were pretty wasted. Fuck, everyone was. I don't understand how you can do that to your body. That's fucked up, you know that, right?"

Mike waggled a finger at Jay, "Hey, man, don't judge, you're the fucking drug dealer."

"Yeah. I deal the shit. I don't do the shit." He held his hands out wide like he was trying to carry an oversized box. "Big. Fucking. Difference."

"I don't do the shit either, man. Meth will fuck you up beyond belief. I'm all natural herbs, mon. Irie!"

Jay shook his head. "You see, this is what's fucked up with this goddamn country. You didn't even consider that the sixteen ounces of alcohol you drank last night was even a drug. Do you realize that you probably left my place with a blood alcohol level high enough to kill a large dog or a small horse? The girl, too. I'm surprised she didn't have to get her stomach pumped."

"Oh, she spent a good amount of time leaning over my toilet this morning, I can assure you. I take small consolation in the fact that it was mostly due to the alcohol poisoning and not the fact that I was standing naked in front of her with a raging hard on while scratching my ass."

"Jesus Christ, man. Too much information. Fuck. I'm not going to be able to get that image out of my head for days."

"Just don't lose your lunch, dude, I might start to get a complex. All right, I gotta go pick up some bong maintenance stuff. I'll meet you at West Side Junkies in ten?"

"Yeah, man, yeah."

The pair visited West Side Junkies and the three other cash houses before returning to Mike's building. In every case the drill was the same. They went to the super's apartment, which had been left vacant at the hand of Mike, into the master bedroom which was fortified and reinforced with steel and in some cases bricks over the window. Jay went into the already opened safe and put the money into a gym bag with dirty clothes on top.

Once safely at Mike's building—also known as The Home Court or "THC" for short—the two men went up to the second floor and Jay opened the door. It had at least four locks holding it shut. A reinforced frame on the inside and a door backing of a quarter-inch steel, not to mention industrial-strength hinges kept it swinging. It was enough to keep the bullets out but it weighed five times the weight of a regular door and required some oomph to get it in motion.

Mike closed and locked the door and Jay led him into the second bedroom. This one was just like all the other ones except smaller. Because he actually spent some time in this apartment when he was not stashing cash, the smaller room was better suited to the job.

Entering the bedroom, Jay dropped the three gym bags he was carrying and Mike dropped his two and took a seat. Jay unlocked the safe and set the money on a large table in the centre of the room. He stacked it neat in columns three high, two across, and two deep. Twelve bundles in total with apparently five grand in each bundle. He pointed to the pile of money. "THC in the house for sixty large. Ten g's over target."

Mike nodded. "Well done, good sir. Take one bundle for yourself."

"You're all right, dude. I'm going to go get me a new juicer."

"Seriously? I hand you five grand and the first thing you think of is a juicer?"

"Shit, dude. We aren't having this conversation twice in one day. You do what you want to do with your money I'll do what I want to do with mine. You dig?"

"You're right, you're right." Mike nodded and opened up a duffle bag and started stacking the money on the table.

The expectation was fifty thousand dollars from each bag. The first three bags came out at fifty grand exactly. The fourth one, from 86th Street Hustle, was in fact, heavy. Fifteen thousand heavy to be exact. Mike carved out seven thousand five hundred and handed it to Jay.

"Make sure there's an appropriate distribution of this, okay?"

"You got it, Mr. Mike."

"Tell 'em I told 'em they're doing a great job, too. A simple thank you goes almost as far as a cash bonus."

"Truth."

Mike started to empty the last bag and furrowed his brow. "Where's this bag from?"

"That one?" He looked in at the t-shirt inside. "That's from the Manic Street Preachers. Did it seem a bit light to you?"

"Hard to say. We picked that one up after the heavy bag. Might have felt light just because the one before it was heavy. How much are they short?"

"Not sure. Gonna have to count it all by hand. Grab a seat."

Mike and Jay opened up the ten bundles and each took five of them. Mike found that the first bundle was short by one hundred and fifty dollars. Jay's first bundle was short seventy-five bucks.

"This is not a good start for our friends on Manic Street."

"No, it's not. This is the part of the job I like the least."

"Yeah, me, too, but we have to do it or the whole system breaks down."

Jay shook his head and continued to count. Mike joined him in silence, whipping off the bills one at a time and placing them on the table in haphazard piles. When he got through his stack, he reached back and folded his hands behind his head. He let out a big sigh. Jay was a little more meticulous with his counting, as if he was actively willing the numbers to come out even. The look on his face indicated they were anything but.

"Well?"

Jay pursed his lips. "Five hundred and fifty missing."

Mike shook his head and put his hands on the table. "I'm six hundred and fifty shy from my stacks. That's twelve hundred light."

Jay tried to push Mike toward the positive. He hated having to come down on a friend he spent his whole life growing up with. "Hey, even after the bonus payouts and this loss you're still a good ten grand heavier than you thought you were gonna be a week ago."

"I see what you're trying to do, Jay, and I appreciate it, I really do, but you know you have to at least rough him up a little."

"Yeah, you're right. Still, that doesn't mean I gotta like it."

"Yeah, it's shitty. We're in this business to make money, not run around all thug-like. Tell ya what? How about I find a guy to give you a hand with it?"

"Give me a hand with it?"

"Yeah, I'll recruit someone for some 'consulting' business. They'll do all the on the ground work and you just have to supervise."

Jay jumped up from the table and did a little dance right then and there while singing the old theme song from *The Jeffersons*. "Movin' on up. Movin' on up. To the East side. In a dee-luxe apartment, in the sky-eye-eye! Oh, yeah, I'm management, baby!"

Mike got up and shot Jay a look that could have indicated he was considering joining in the dancing but instead he pulled out his cell phone and made a call.

"Dave, it's Mike. Look, I need a particular set of skills for a quick smash and grab. No, not where—*who*. Yeah, that kind of smash and grab. Look, bill it to Thomas, okay? I need my hands clean on this one. Yeah, no, he doesn't know and it shall stay that way. Understood? Perfect. Thanks."

Mike turned to look at Jay who was staring at him with his jaw slack.

"Dude, that's cold. I'm not sure whether to respect you or slap you upside the head."

Mike shrugged. "Better him than me, besides, that's what he gets for being slumlord of the year. I mean, look at those buildings. They're a fucking disaster. He doesn't give a shit so long as he gets the rent checks."

Jay nodded in agreement. "Hey man, you're the boss. Let's pack this shit up and get it to the bank."

SATURDAY, JULY 8, 6:00 P.M.

Thomas hung up the phone with Mike and plopped himself down into his leather recliner. Brittany muted the television and crossed her legs on the couch, grabbing her toes like she used to when she was a little girl.

"Oh, I see how this is going to play out."

"I know we just had a conversation about money, but I thought that maybe there could be some way for me to get a little extra cash, you know, if I were to work for it or something."

"Mmmhuh. Possibly. Do you have any particular skills that would be of use? Can you type on something that isn't your phone? Do you know how to clean?"

"Daddy, I'm being serious. If I wanted cash, how would you suggest I go about getting more of it?"

"Get a job."

Brittany folded her arms. "That's what I'm trying to do!"

Thomas leaned forward. "Listen to me. What you're doing is asking me to find you a job. What you need to do is get off your ass and find yourself a job. Here's a lesson for you, and it won't cost you a dime. Finding a job is the hardest job you're ever going to have."

"It can't be that hard, can it? There must be something I can do at the office. Some menial job or something that no one likes doing."

"We have people doing those jobs already. I've got Jenny who works for me, and any of the other executives have their own assistants. They do everything for us from making coffee to getting our dry cleaning to scheduling and paperwork. You want me to just fire Jenny, a job that she earned and works hard at improving at every day, so I can just hand it to you. Explain that to Jenny and any of the people that depend on her for that job."

"But *Daddy!*"

Thomas stared her down for several seconds before speaking.

"That tone is not helping your cause, I can guarantee you that. Concentrate on your school. Enjoy your off times with your friends—which I pay for, I might add. Worry about money after you graduate and before I die. On the either end of those two things your life is pretty grand."

Brenda trotted past the living room on her way to the kitchen. She was trying to affix a large diamond stud earring into her earlobe. "Listen to your father."

"Mom!"

"Your mother agrees with me and that almost never happens, so it seems like this should be advice that you heed."

Brittany stormed off to her room, returned with a small backpack slung over her shoulder, and stomped toward the apartment door.

"Just where do you think you're going?"

"I'm going to the art opening, probably staying up all night, then spending some time at Melissa's."

She reached down and grabbed a pen and sticky note from the table beside the door. "This is her number. It's her cell. You can try to reach her in the event you try to reach me and can't get through to my cell."

"And what are the chances I'll be able to get you on your cell?"

She looked over her shoulder as she walked into the penthouse outer hallway. "Not very good." She shut the door behind her.

Brenda came out from the kitchen, her earring where it should be and a small chocolate wafer between her fingers. "That went well."

Thomas sat back in his chair, deflated. "What would you have me do, Brenda? Just throw money at her until she can't stop smiling?"

She took a nibble of her treat and pointed the jagged remains of the wafer in his general direction. "It's been working with me for more than a decade."

SATURDAY, JULY 8, 8:00 P.M.

Mike made his way over to Thomas's house with a handful of munchies and a six-pack of beer. After some pleasantries with the security guard he enjoyed some quality time with his favorite friend and his favorite hockey team. Partway through the game, his host excused himself to head to the washroom. He knew he only had a minute, so Mike jumped over the couch and ran down the hall, around the corner past Mother's room, and into Brittany's. Opening her nightstand, he shuffled stuff around looking for any sign of drugs or money. Both night side tables contained nothing but lipgloss and random do-dads and whatchamacallits he didn't have any interest in.

He slid the top drawer of her dresser open and shuffled a few bras out of the way and all he found were more bras. Opening the next drawer down, he encountered an avalanche of underwear, tossed in with what must have been reckless abandon. Checking over his shoulder to ensure the coast was still clear, he reached to the back of the drawer and pulled out a pair of ordinary black cotton underpants. He shrugged his shoulders and whispered, "I guess these will have to do," and stuffed them into the pocket of his jeans. He closed the drawer and made a quick exit out of the bedroom and back to the couch.

SATURDAY, JULY 8, 10:00 P.M.

Mike exited the elevator in the lobby and his phone notified him he had voicemail. He shook his head in disbelief. He cleared his throat loudly to draw attention to himself. "Hey Mitch, how come you have the fanciest elevator in New York and you can't get a cell signal in it?"

He shrugged and didn't so much as bother to look up from his magazine. "It's one of the greatest mysteries of the Universe."

"Dick."

Mike picked up the message. *"Hey boss, it's Jay. I got a request here from little B asking for an advance. How you want me to play it?"* Mike hung up and dialed Jay as he exited the building, ignoring Mitch's glare. "Jay, how much of an advance does she want?"

"A lot. She wants to treat a butt-load of her friends to a special time. The good stuff, too, not the usual stuff we hand out on the corner, you know."

"A fistfull of the private reserve is going to cost her extra. She there now?"

"Yeah, she's around."

Mike stopped outside the entrance to the subway so he could continue the conversation. The subway rivaled the fancy elevator for worst reception in the city. "Find her and put her on."

"All right. Hang on."

Mike heard lots of talking and music, but it didn't sound like a club. After a full minute he heard Jay's muffled voice away from the phone talking to a girl.

"He wants to talk to you."

The girl didn't want to take the phone. "He knows I'm good for it. Can't I just have it?"

Jay was insistent, like the good foot soldier Mike expected him to be. "He. Wants. To. Talk. To. You."

A girl's whine echoed through the phone. "Yeah?"

He cracked his neck and took a deep breath. "Is that any way to talk to the guy who's about to make your night a memorable one?"

"Look, I don't want to make a big deal out of this. You know I'm good for it."

"I'm not so sure you are. From what Jay tells me—you do know he and I talk quite frequently, don't you?" He paused to see if she would reply. When she didn't, he continued. "Don't you?"

"Yeah. I know you talk."

"Good. Then you know I know about last night when you took out an advance for half of the house party guests, plus who knows how much alcohol. I'm not convinced you're liquid enough to even pay back that, let alone another advance—of the good stuff, no less."

"Look, you know I can get the money. It'll take a couple days, but I can get it. Plus, we have our, what did you call it? Our little arrangement."

Mike reached into his pocket and felt the soft cotton underpants. "Fine. One more small advance at Jay's discretion, but—but—it's going to cost a little extra, on account of me being such a nice guy. Do you understand?"

She paused for several seconds before responding. *"Oh, I understand. Do you?"*

He never allowed for buyer's remorse before sealing a deal. Never. "It's crystal clear, babe. It's settled then. It better not get ugly."

"It won't."

"We'll see. Put Jay back on."

"So, where we at?"

"Give her what she needs from the good stuff, but not a morsel more, and get me a total from last night, too. I want to make sure I invoice this properly."

"Sure thing, boss. Anything else you need? Lots of fine ladies here tonight."

Mike fondled the panties one more time. "Nah, I'm good here."

CHAPTER*FOURTEEN*

Mike rolled over in bed and reached around for his bong. Realizing he left it in the other room, he sighed and debated getting out of bed or lying there for another couple hours to get some more sleep. He looked over at the two pairs of underpants hanging from his night side table lamp and decided to stay in bed. Rolling back over so he wasn't facing the window with the ripped curtain hanging from a bent metal rod, he daydreamt of a threesome between Brittany, Melissa, and himself. Just as his imagination was really starting to work, the phone rang. He briefly considered letting it go to voicemail but he checked the call display first. Seeing that it was Jay, he tabled his fantasy and answered the call.

"I'm working here. This better be good."

"Good morning to you, too. Listen I got a total for you from B."

Mike sat up and rubbed his hand through his hair. "I'm listening. How deep is she in?"

"Deep. About four grand. It was mostly teeners and a few eight balls, but once they got a taste of the good stuff, that's all any of them wanted. I had to lie and say we were out just to get her to stop."

"What'd you do that for?"

"Just smart business, Mike. There's no way she's coming up with that much

cash, not with her circumstances being what they are. I don't care how rich her daddy is, he don't give her shit. How much is an alternate form of payment worth to you anyway? Not that much, I can guarantee it. No sense in just giving away choice product at this point."

Mike's shoulders slumped and he let out a large breath. "Yeah, I hear ya. Shit. This is why I like to only deal with people I don't have any connection to, you know?"

"Yeah, well that's one of them golden rules, or cardinal rules, or some shit. There are rules with colors involved and that's one of them. Same as no talking about politics, religion, or money with folks. Never ends well."

"I think it's cardinal rule. Anyway, yeah, this might not end well for her. It will for me, but long term this is damaging. Aw, fuck it. Okay, has my guy called you about the smash and grab?"

"Yeah, he called."

"Look, I sense your discomfort with all this, but what would you like me to do?"

There was a long pause. *"Mike, I respect you, you know that, and it's only because I think we make a good team and are tight that I would ever dream of saying this—"*

"Jesus Christ, man, just spit it the hell out. You have my permission to speak freely."

"Right, it's just that you're not doing B like that, and she's downright stealing from you. I just don't like to see a brother receive that kind of treatment is all."

Mike let out a fit of booming laughter. "Shit, dude, you think I'm getting all racist on this shit? First, I'm a little insulted. I'm *more* than a little insulted. Second, you want to know the biggest difference between your boy and the girl, aside from the fucking obvious?" Silence. "I'll fucking tell you. He's my fucking employee and she's my fucking customer. She gets preferential treatment because if I play it right, she gives me money and tells her cute little friends and then they give me money. If I don't come down hard on your boy, what's he gonna do?" More silence. "I'll fucking tell you. He's going to take more of my money. Now granted, he might not be keeping it for himself. Maybe he's a baby daddy, maybe he has a sick mama, or maybe he's giving it to fucking charity. Who the fuck knows? Who the fuck cares? He took money from me and no amount of me being nice is going to get my money back and get more in my pocket on top of it."

"You're right, Mikey." His voice was less tentative.

"I know."

"Sorry for questioning you."

"Stop being such a pussy. When's my guy coming to get you?"

"I'm meeting him around the corner in twenty minutes. I'm going to walk, so I gotta get going."

"All right, whatever you do, just listen to him."

"Shit, dude, now you're telling the black drug dealer how to be gangsta?"

"Touché. Look, it's just that he has a certain finesse, that's all. Pay attention and do what he says. You might learn something."

"All right. I'll call you back when we're done and let you know how it went."

"That's all I ask, Jay. Thank you."

"Oh, Mike, one more thing."

"Yes, grasshopper?"

"What if my guy coughs up the cash? Does he still get a talking to?"

"Yes." he hung up before there could be any more discussion on the matter.

SUNDAY, JULY 9, 10:00 A.M.

After riding the subway for a while and drinking two large coffees, Brittany arrived at Melissa's apartment. With her knees pressed tight, she knocked on the door. Melissa answered and she barged in and headed straight for the washroom. Dropping her pants to the floor, she sat down and peed with the door open. "Thanks again for letting me crash for a bit." She checked her phone to see if either of her parents had called her. Neither did.

"No worries. What's the deal, anyway? Your texts were kinda—I dunno—cryptic and shit."

Brittany stood and hiked her pants up before flushing. She started washing her hands. "Ugh. My fucking dad."

Melissa sat down on her couch and wrapped all the limbs she could around a huge pillow, which ended up being both arms and one and a half legs. "Duh, I kind of figured, especially since your mom is covering for you now. What kind of bullshit did he say or do this time? Did he take away your cards? That would totally suck."

She joined her friend on the couch, attempting a similar full body wrap around another giant pillow. "Almost. He won't give me a job."

"What?"

"He won't give me a job."

"You asked him for a job? *You?* You asked your father if you could work for him? You? *Work* for *him?*"

"Yes! Jesus. I need the fucking money and he's not about giving me cash. I figured if I showed some initiative and promised to work he'd at least give me a loan or an advance or something."

Melissa's eyes widened. "Shit, I take it the whole conversation went south."

"Yeah, hence my presence on your couch. I'm not sure what I'm going to do."

"How much do you need? I could lend you some money. I've got some savings kicking around."

"I could never ask you for money. That's not why I'm here."

Melissa put her hand on Brittany's arm. "I know, and you're not asking, I'm offering."

"It's too much, plus I don't have a clue how long it will take me to pay you back."

"Shit, Brit, just tell me how much you owe."

Brittany sighed and stared at the floor, picking at a hangnail on her thumb. "Thousands."

Melissa just about choked on her next breath. "Jesus fuck. To *who?* For *what?* And what do you mean by 'thousands?' How plural is that word?"

"Jay, or rather, his boss and the classy gentleman who's probably been jerking off all day holding a pair of your underwear."

She scrunched up her nose, stuck out her tongue, and pretended to gag. "Not one of my finer moments, but we do what we gotta and my wallet's got a lotta." She pretends to slap bills off one hand with her other one. "I guess that answers the 'for what' question, too."

"Yeah, I kind of opened the floodgates last night at this art show opening. I was already in for a little bit from Friday night and I just got overly generous with all the art snobs."

Melissa reached forward and pointed her finger towards Brittany's heart. "If they don't like you for what's in here, then they're not your real friends."

Brittany smiled for the first time in several hours. "Says the girl who had sex with my drug dealer's supplier, who also happens to have an arrangement with me, *and* who also happens be my dad's best friend."

"I didn't know your arrangement was exclusive, girl. And at least he used condoms."

Brittany raised an eyebrow. "It's not that and you know it. He's an easy mark and not bad-looking for an old guy. Wait, what? Condoms? *Plural?* Was he double-bagging it to protect himself from your toxic vag?"

Melissa took a swing at her with a smaller throw pillow. "No, you bitch. We had sex three times. Well, two-and-a-half."

"He said that, too!"

"That kiss-and-tell motherfucker! He—well, *we*—passed out in the middle of the third go, apparently. It must have been some pretty active sex, though, because my twat is aching. It hadn't got a workout that thorough since I changed the batteries on Mr. Pickles."

"Mr. Pickles?"

"My bestest and most loyalest friend in the whole world. My big green vibrator sent down from the heavens by God himself to ensure that I get a good night's sleep so long as I can find 'D' cell batteries at Costco."

Brittany laughed and covered her mouth as a gigglesnort escaped. "I am so jealous. Not of the fact that you fucked Mike, but that you can use power tools in the bedroom. I live with my parents so anything that makes noise is strictly out of the question."

"That sucks."

"It truly does. I have to smother myself with a pillow when a good one hits just so I don't wake everyone up."

The two girls sat in silence for a few seconds, uncertain where to take the conversation now.

"How many thousands again?"

"Four, plus he said that it would cost extra. I never did settle with him on what my alternate payments are worth. I've always just kinda winged it."

Melissa grabbed her laptop and started typing. She leaned over to look. "Whatcha typing?"

"I'm logging into my bank. I can e-transfer you some money."

"Mel, you don't have to do that. It'll work out."

"Look, Brit. I've got the money and you need the money. As much as you have an arrangement with him if you can square up with a bit of cash it'll take some of the pressure off and he won't get any ideas about taking more than he deserves."

"You're making a good point."

"Plus, I will still have a few bucks in the bank in case I need it. At least this way you can give him a good amount, even if it's not all of it and then get on with your day not owing the loser anything."

"I couldn't. You can't…."

"You can, and I just did. Let's go to the bank machine now. We can both take out five hundred and five hundred again tomorrow. You can give him two grand tomorrow and sort out the rest however you see fit. At least this way you've got options."

"Options are good. I really should start paying attention in class. My business plans need a little refining."

"That's why you've got me. Okay, let's get to the ATM before it gets too late. I don't want to be walking around with that kind of cash after it gets dark."

MONDAY, JULY 10, 12:10 A.M.

The girls returned from their second trip to the ATM flush with cash. Melissa rifled through her desk drawer and pulled out four white envelopes. "This will have to do for now." She took her wad of twenties and put them in an envelope, sealing it with a lick and making a face in protest of the taste of the terrible glue. Brittany did the same with her stack of bills, only she handed it to Melissa to seal.

"No fucking way, I just gave you two grand. You can lick your own goddamn envelope."

"If I could do that I'd never leave the house!"

"Oh, my god, you're such a perv!"

Brittany pointed to Melissa's bedroom. "Says the girl with the vag-busting sexual power tool in her night side table. Now seriously, just lick this."

"That's what she said."

"Argh. You're so juvenile sometimes." She snatched the envelope back. "Fine I'll do it myself."

"That is also what she said."

Brittany sealed the envelope and took it with the other one, stuffing them in her bag with the few pieces of clothing she packed before she left. "Do you think we should write the amount on the outside or something?"

"You're not paying a fucking hydro bill! These are drug dealers. You'll hand them the money, tell them how much it is and how you'll be handling the rest and that's that."

"Options."

Melissa put her arm around Brittany. "That's right. Look, let's call it a night. I'll make up the futon in the living room for you."

Brittany ran scenario after scenario through her head, and in spite of all but two of them working out in her favor, she tossed and turned for several minutes. The key was going to be impressing upon dear Mike the value in her proposition.

Outside, the temperature and humidity were rising even as the night settled in and the noise of the city seemed louder than usual in the warm, dense air. She slid off the futon, stood up, and shut the window.

Settling back in bed the quiet was welcome but once she stopped shifting her pillow under her head, she heard a noise coming from the other side of the wall. "Ah, that must be the voice of Mr. Pickles."

She covered her head under the pillow, not quite in the mood to hear her best friend in the throes of passion with her favorite battery-operated assistant. Still, the toy was loud and her attempts at keeping her moans muted were not one hundred percent successful. She got up and opened the window again, this time wider than before. A wave of warm, humid air wafted into the apartment along with the street noise of one of the world's busiest cities. She decided to let her friend enjoy her pre-bedtime routine and she lay back and concentrated on sounds from the streets below. The symphony of the city put her to sleep.

*CHAPTER*FIFTEEN

Brittany awoke to the sound of a car accident outside and a lot of yelling. She popped out of bed, her back aching from a poor night's sleep on a cheap futon and looked out the window. Two taxicabs collided in an effort to pick up a fare and the drivers were going toe-to-toe in the middle of the road. As she watched, the poor person who wanted a taxi wandered off around the corner. She walked down the hall and heard the sound of water running in the shower. She wandered into Melissa's room in search of a long t-shirt to throw on over her minimalist pajamas and spotted Mr. Pickles on the night side table. Her jaw dropped at the sight of it. It was positively frightening, but she couldn't bring herself to look away. "It's no wonder you couldn't contain yourself last night, Mel. That thing is fucking insane." Wandering past the closet, she spotted a long, loose-fitting t-shirt on the floor and threw it on. Exiting the room, she glanced one more time over her shoulder at Mr. Pickles and made her way to the kitchen to brew some coffee.

Melissa joined her in the kitchen dressed in a Ramones t-shirt and pair of ripped jeans. She was still massaging her hair into a towel to dry it off. "Oh, you made coffee. You're such a lifesaver. I slept like a rock but could have stayed in bed all day. I need a jolt to get my ass in gear."

Brittany cradled her large mug of coffee in her hands. "I bet you slept."

Melissa cocked an eyebrow. "What's that supposed to mean?"

Brittany put her coffee down and her hands between her legs, pretending to hold a vibrator. *"Buzzzzzzzzzzzzzzzzz."* She made orgasm faces and threw her head back in fake ecstasy and convulsing while twitching in her chair.

Melissa's cheeks turned fifty shades of pink. "Oh. Em. *Gee.* You heard that?"

"The whole *neighborhood* heard that. I went to open the window and a cabbie thought someone was trying to hail him."

"Why didn't you say something? Oh my god, I'm mortified."

She shrugged her shoulders. "I didn't want to disturb your routine."

Melissa sat down with a giant mug of coffee. "I'm so sorry, did I keep you up?"

"Nah, don't sweat it. My brain was racing anyway. I slept like a giant pile of shit." She took a healthy gulp of her morning caffeine.

"Yeah, about that. What's the plan? Where are we going to meet after?"

Brittany raised both her eyebrows. "We?"

"Yeah, we. You don't think I'm going to let you do this alone do you? Not all of it, at least"

"You don't think I'm going to let you come, do you? You're my best friend, but I don't think tag-teaming my dealer is the best idea." She put her mug down with enough force to splash some over the edge and onto the table.

"Listen, Brit, it's not safe, no matter how you slice it. Here you've got an opportunity at least to make it safer. Think about it for a minute. Your business model to this point has been relatively small-time. If it was like all those times before it would be the same arrangement as before. This time, he set up a separate meeting and asked for cash."

"I know it's not that safe, but it's not like they're going to kill me. How would Mike explain that one to my dad? 'Oh sorry about that, Thomas. Your daughter owed me a few grand for some drugs and a couple grand and a quickie weren't enough to pay it off so I popped a cap in her ass.' That won't ever happen."

She folded her arms. "But at the same time you don't want me going with you because...?"

Brittany hung her head and sighed. "Because it's not safe." She added,

"FOR YOU!" before Melissa had the chance to jump in. "It's not safe for you. Thomas Van Steen isn't your dad. You are absolutely nothing to these guys and who knows, Mike might be pissed you pulled that stunt the other night."

"So when I do it it's a stunt but when you do it it's just smart business?"

"That's not what I mean and you know it. Tell me, when he checked his wallet after you left how much money was in it?"

"He didn't have that much anyway."

"Not the point. You didn't just exchange sex for alcohol and drugs, you literally stole money from a drug dealer's wallet."

"Okay, how about I come with you but wait around the corner at the coffee shop?"

"Fine. As for me, I've got an idea that'll keep everything under control."

"Oh, do tell, Miss Evil Fucking Genius who got herself into this mess with her superior judgement."

"Ouch, that stings. Okay, here's the deal. I call and tell him I have the money. I won't say that I don't have all of it. This way he'll not feel any need to prepare. I tell him to meet me in the stairwell of my building. Mike will be able to get into the building by saying he's going up to see my dad or forgot something when he last visited or some shit like that."

"How is this safer? How is hanging out in a stairwell—in your own condo I might add—keeping everything under control? It only takes a second for shit to go south and now you've just added the extra bonus of your family and neighbors finding out you're in tight with the Mike and Jay drug cartel."

"You don't know what I know about the stairwells in my building."

"They're way slower than the elevator but walking them gives you a tight ass and nice calves?"

"No! Well, yes. But no! The stairwells in my building have cameras. A fuckload of them. One on every goddamn floor with a feed to the security desk and into the elevators. I'll be on camera the whole time and I'll make sure Mike knows it."

"Jesus. That's some creepy shit. Why the hell is your building so wired?"

"Don't get me started. Some old hag on the fourth floor sees things. She's paranoid someone's going to jump her and steal her purse. She got a bunch of the other tenants in a tizzy over it and they all voted to have the condo board spent a buttload of money with all the cameras and shit. I don't pay the condo fees, so whatever, but it's going to come in real handy today I tell you what."

"Your parents won't see?"

"Dad will be at work and mom never turns them on. She thinks they're creepy and an invasion of privacy."

Melissa pondered the situation by staring into her massive mug of breakfast beverage. "I don't like it, but if you're going to be on camera the whole time that's got to be safer than just some random street corner, or worse," she shuddered visibly at the thought, "at Mike's apartment."

"That bad, eh?"

"Yeah, you have no idea. I've taken like ten showers since Saturday morning when I got home and today."

"Jesus."

The two girls sat in silence and finished their coffees. Brittany got up and put her empty mug in the sink, on her way to the living room. She dug into her bag and pulled out her cell phone. Checking the time, she dialed Mike. It went to voicemail after the fourth ring. "Mike, it's B. I've got what you're looking for. Meet me in the east stairwell of my building on the fifth floor at twelve thirty. If I don't hear back from you I'll assume you're okay with that." She hung up and looked over to Melissa. "I'm going to shower and then we'll go get some more cash. I'll subway back to my place from the ATM."

"Perfect. Do you want a coffee for after your rendezvous?"

"Yeah sure, that'll work. Just don't let them see you. I don't want Mike getting any big ideas about a sober repeat of Friday."

CHAPTER SIXTEEN

Jay stopped at the door that exited onto the fourth floor and kept an eye on the stairwell. Mike continued up and met Brittany on the landing. Thomas pressed the button to turn on the sound. Before Mike had a chance to say anything Brittany held up the four envelopes full of cash. Mike took them from her and put them into his coat pocket.

"I can get you the rest by Wednesday. I reached my ATM withdrawal limit. Or, we can set up our usual alternate." She took a step forward and ran her finger up his arm.

Mike tilted his head back and inhaled deeply. "Hmm. I thought you said you had the money."

"I do, I just can't get it out of my account. Look, I just handed you a lot of cash. I've got the rest. Or…." She took another step forward and her toes touched his. She slid her hand down to his pants waist and below his belt buckle. "We can meet at our usual spot. I'm not busy for the rest of the afternoon."

Thomas lifted his hand to take a swing at the last unbroken monitor and thought better of it. His hand was already bleeding and he didn't want to break it. He needed to be able to pull the trigger so he could kill his best friend.

"Look, B, I'm in the drug business, not the loan business, and you've overextended your credit. I need the money this time."

"I know you're not in the loan business. I know. I got carried away. Look, I'll get you the rest when I can take money out of the ATM again, and I'll keep up my end of our usual agreement to cover any extra interest or whatever."

Mike stared at Brittany for a second and then touched her hair. She pulled her head away and turned her head to face the camera. "Cameras, man. We're already pushing our luck. You have as much to lose here as I do, probably more."

"I took care of the cameras. Your dad really ought to pay Mitch a better salary. Kid's super easy to bribe."

"Well, then." She put her arms around his neck and pressed her body against his. "I guess we can settle up right here."

Mike dug his hand into his pants pocket and pulled out her underwear. He held them up and let them dangle from an extended index finger. "I might have taken out a teensy advance."

"You little pervert." She smiled. "You should have grabbed the ones off the floor if you wanted the full effect."

"I know, but I was hoping I'd get the opportunity to get the full effect in person." He reached down and cupped her groin with his hand. She let out a gasp and returned the favor. He spun her around and pushed her against the wall.

Thomas screamed at the monitor. "No! No no no no no no!" He paced back and forth, pulling at his hair, spittle flying from his mouth. "You sick fuck! You sick fuck! You. Sick. Fuck!"

Mike unbuttoned his jeans and pulled them down just enough for him to expose himself. He reached into his back pocket, took out a condom, and started to put it on. Brittany lifted her hips and slid her yoga pants and underwear down to her ankles. She backed up into him and wiggled her bum.

Thomas took a run at the monitor from the other side of the elevator and threw an elbow into it, sending glass spraying everywhere and turning the screen into a mess of green and blue wiggly lines. He could still make out the sounds of grunts from Mike and moans of pleasure coming from his daughter.

After a couple minutes, there was an eerie moment of quiet before Brittany's voice crackled through the speaker. "Whoa, Mikey, I'm beginning to think Melissa knew what she was doing when she picked you."

"I have my moments."

"Here, let me trade you for the advance you took. These will have more of that lived-in feel when you use them to tug one out later. Plus, you snatched my favorite pair and I'm not ready to see them go just yet."

"Fine by me. When can I see you again?"

"Whenever I need something. Don't worry I've got your number."

Thomas collapsed to the floor of the elevator. Pieces of glass dug into his backside as he slumped into the corner. Tears flowed down his cheeks. Snot dripped from his nose. Blood oozed out from his knuckles and elbow.

The sound of Brittany's ring tone echoed through the stairwell and into the elevator. "Oh hey! Yeah, it's all good. Tall soy latte. See you in five."

Thomas got to his knees and switched the audio back to the lobby. His daughter emerged from the stairwell humming a song he heard blasting from her room every morning. She got to the lobby and Mitch was still sitting at the security desk. He didn't even look in her direction as she made her way to the exit.

Nikki emerged from under the desk. "Was that Thomas's daughter?"

Mitch glanced to the main entrance and then back to the cash sitting on top of the stack that Nikki brought him. "Nope." He flipped on the monitor and typed a few keys to start the camera recording for floor five again.

Thomas sat on the floor of the elevator, crying, and unable to get the strength to stand up. He looked at his watch. Forty-five minutes had passed since the lights went out. He closed his eyes and let out a deep exhale before passing out.

EPILOGUE

THOMAS

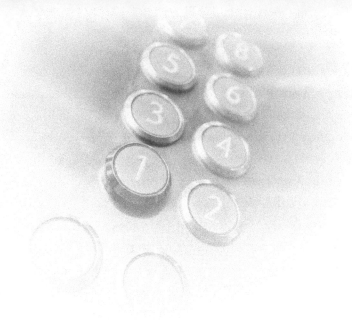

MONDAY, JULY 10, 3:00 P.M.

Thomas opened his eyes and checked his watch. It had been three hours since the power went out and the elevator's emergency lights and the two monitors that were not completely shattered cast a dull glow. Mitch paced in the foyer near the front entrance and Nikki stood beside the security desk. Thomas watched him walk to the front door and hold it open for a pair of paramedics pushing a gurney. He put his head in his hands and started to sob. "I'm so sorry, Mother. I'm so sorry."

He looked up at the screen and caught sight of a foot before it disappeared into an elevator. Thomas's was still dark save the one emergency light. He checked his watch and it still read three hours since the power went out. His watch had stopped. He pulled himself to his feet, checked the monitor, and pressed the sound button on and off. There was no longer any sound coming from the speaker. After several minutes, he saw one paramedic come into view. He walked over to Mitch and said something but he couldn't read lips. Mitch nodded and the paramedic walked back toward the elevators. Nikki whispered something into Mitch's ear and he followed the paramedic toward the elevator.

The two paramedics wheeled the gurney out of the elevator and into view and Thomas's sobbing became uncontrollable as he realized there was a body bag on top of it. Mitch leaned in and said something to the paramedic and the young man shook his head. Mitch held up his hands and pleaded with him, hitting the back of one hand into the palm of the other. The paramedic nodded and unzipped the body bag.

Thomas's knees buckled as he watched his own face appear between the folds of the bag. His t-shirt was torn and the electrodes from the portable defibrillator were still stuck to his chest. Mitch reached down into the body bag and took Thomas's keys out from his pocket. He removed the safety deposit box key and clutched it in his palm. He walked it back to the security desk where he pulled out the logbook from under the counter and pretended to add an entry. Nikki slid over beside him and he slipped her the key when no one was watching. The paramedics zipped up the body bag and wheeled Thomas outside.

In the elevator, Thomas stared at the screen, and the orange emergency light in the corner started to flicker. He felt a jolt from the elevator kicking into motion again.

He didn't have to look to know which direction it was headed.

—

Upstairs, Thomas's mother opened her eyes and lifted up her oxygen mask. "Cereal."

ANDREW IS A 40-SOMETHING married father of two living in Cambridge, Ontario. He says that his first published work was Losing Vern as part of the *Orange Karen: A Tribute to a Warrior* anthology. In reality, it was a 500-word anecdote about the time he lit himself on fire. That story made it into the third installment of the Darwin Awards books.

Fire is not the only foe for Andrew. He has received several severe concussions and a few "minor" ones, the last coming in the summer of 2011. It goes without saying that he is one hundred percent on board with head protection and brain health.

Not all his distinctions are as dubious as appearing in a Darwin Awards book. There was the time he did a trick on stage with Penn & Teller. He had a minute of time the Super Dave Osborne show. He scored a game-winning goal at Maple Leaf Gardens and even "sold" music to filmmaker Kevin Smith. He was even given a whole three seconds of non-speaking airtime in a TV commercial. And who could forget when he appeared as a fighting homeless man in a rap video.

His first published book, *Bent But Not Broken*, a story about his daughter's scoliosis surgery is available now. He currently blogs, is writing his next novel, is a huge fan of golf, hockey, science, equality, and the Oxford comma.

Andrew sometimes lets his love of attention override common sense. You can find evidence of this pretty much anywhere you can find Andrew.

www.potatochipmath.com

...rmation can be obtained
...sting.com
...USA
...44220421
...LV00005B/379